CURSE OF QUANTRILL

In the American Civil War, Quantrill was a strange man who refused to admit defeat. A Southern fanatic, he and his band of riders fought a guerrilla war against the Northern Union. Alongside Jud Hawkins, he continued his rebellion even when he discovered that the war was over. But Quantrill eventually realized that the aim of his raiders had become distorted. Now he must wage his own war, which would be a grim and final battle to the death.

CARL MADDOX

CURSE OF QUANTRILL

WORCESTERSHIRE COUNTY COUNCIL
CULTURAL SERVICES

Complete and Unabridged

LINFORD
Leicester

First published in Great Britain in 2000

First Linford Edition
published 2007

British Library CIP Data

Maddox, Carl, 1919 –
    Curse of Quantrill.—Large print ed.—
Linford western library
    1. Western stories
    2. Large type books
    I. Title II. Steven, John. Night raiders
823.9'14 [F]

ISBN 978–1–84617–739–2

Published by
F. A. Thorpe (Publishing)
Anstey, Leicestershire

Set by Words & Graphics Ltd.
Anstey, Leicestershire
Printed and bound in Great Britain by
T. J. International Ltd., Padstow, Cornwall

This book is printed on acid-free paper

1

He rode into town at sundown, arriving just as the evening shadows crept from the east to soften the harsh outlines of the sun-scorched desert. He looked tired, slumped in his saddle as if he had driven himself to the very limit of his endurance. The horse, too, a big gelding, dust covered and foam speckled, seemed ready to drop in its tracks with sheer exhaustion and, as rider and horse wended their slow way through the dusty streets, many curious eyes stared at them.

Jud Hawkins was aware of those eyes and cursed the bad luck which had made such speed and hard travel necessary. He drew rein at the livery stable, called to a groom, and dug coins from his pocket as the man took the reins.

'Take care of him, mister. Rub him

down and walk him for a spell. Go easy on the water and feed him the best in the house!'

'I know my business.' The man, a sour-faced oldster, held out his hand. 'A dollar a day livery charge. How long will you leave him?'

'I don't know.' Jud handed the man two dollars. 'One for the horse and one for yourself. I'll drop in sometime tomorrow.'

'Sure.' The groom smiled and patted the neck of the horse. 'I'll treat him right. You want your stuff?'

'Take care of it for me, will you?' Jud glanced at his bed-roll, saddle-bags and scabbarded rifle. 'I'll call back later for what I need. All right?'

'Leave it with me.' The groom glanced with professional interest at the gelding. 'Come far?'

'A fair piece.'

'You staying in town?'

'Maybe.'

'If you want a good hotel try the Royal.' The man was obviously both curious and eager to please. Jud guessed that money was as tight in Illinois as it was in most of the North; his tip had loosened the groom's tongue.

'I'll remember it,' said Jud. 'Who shall I say sent me?'

'Zeke, Zeke Murphy.' The groom sucked at his teeth. 'The best damn horse-handler in Springfield if I say so myself.'

'I'm not arguing,' said Jud mildly. He glanced towards the street thronged with men wearing the blue uniforms of the Northern Army. 'Soldiers keep you busy?'

'Not so's you'd notice.' Zeke spat in the dust. 'You from the West?'

'Wyoming,' lied Jud. 'You?'

'Texas.' Zeke shrugged. 'That was a long time ago. My Pa got killed in the Indian raids and my Ma brought me up here when I was ten. That was a long time ago.' He peered at Jud. 'You know, you look as if you might be a Texas man yourself. Are you?'

'Maybe.' Jud turned as the tramp of marching feet echoed from the street and a file of soldiers passed by. They were young men mostly, with a sprinkle of grizzled veterans as NCOs, and at their head rode a young officer resplendent in his new uniform, his sabre polished to match the glistening perfection of his holster and boots. Jud watched them march from view.

'Going to the station,' explained Zeke. 'They're shipping out all the time.' He spat again. 'I wonder how many of them will live through their first meeting with the Rebs?'

He shrugged and led the horse into the livery stable and Jud, glad at getting away from the talkative oldster, made his way down the street towards the hotel the old man had named.

He registered as Sam Calloway, a commercial traveller, and insisted on a room with a bath.

'Bath?' The receptionist blinked. 'There's a bath house down the street, sir.'

'I want a room with one of them fancy baths,' insisted Jud. 'I've the money to pay for it and I reckon I'm going to have it.'

'Yes, sir.' The clerk, a thin, pale-faced man, licked his lips as he stared at the tall, hard-faced man on the other side of the counter. 'The best we can do is to send up a bath and have it filled for you, will that do?'

'Sure.' Jud smiled and relaxed a little. 'You see, son, I've been riding a long way and I'm full of dust. I want to wash clean and I want to do it in luxury.' He smiled even wider. 'Don't look so surprised, even though I may look and smell like a Westerner, that doesn't mean I've no taste for the finer things.'

'No, sir.' The clerk hesitated. 'What did you say you were travelling in, sir?'

'I didn't.'

'No, sir, sorry, sir.' The clerk flushed. 'That will be ten dollars a day, Mr Calloway. Bath will be five dollars extra. How long do you intend to stay?'

'A day, maybe more.' Jud dug into his

pockets and produced a roll of green-backs. He counted off fifteen dollars, dropped them on the counter, and tucked the rest back into his pocket.

'Number twenty-two.' The clerk rang a bell and a stoop-shouldered negro came towards them. 'Escort this gentleman to number twenty-two, Rastus.'

'Yas, suh. Yo baggage, suh?'

'I'll bring it in later,' said Jud. He stared at the clerk. 'I want that bath, son, and I want it in a hurry. Get it?'

'Yes, sir.' The clerk sighed as he watched the new guest follow the servant up the wide stairs towards his room. A man, dressed in broadcloth and riding boots, folded his newspaper and approached the desk.

'My key.'

'Yes, Mr Thorne, right away, sir.' The clerk reached behind him and dropped it on the counter. 'Did you ever see anything like that in your life?'

'Like what?'

'That man who just came in. From the look of him I'd say he was a cowpuncher or maybe a prospector. Spurs, six-gun, knife, the works. Yet he tells me that he's a commercial traveller and demands a bath. What line of goods could a man like that be selling?'

'Can't you guess?' Thorne smiled, the lines deepening in his face. 'Springfield owns more than a railhead, you know, or have you forgotten?'

'Rifles!' The clerk frowned. 'But surely the Army is taking all we can make?'

'Yes, the new models, but don't forget the old stocks. I expect the gentleman has been selling them to the traders in the West.'

'I see.' The clerk smiled as though relieved at the simple solution to what had worried him. 'I'd better send up his bath. If you will excuse me?'

Thorne nodded and, taking his key, went up to his room. He waited for perhaps an hour and then, cautiously, he left his room and walked down the corridor to number twenty-two. Swiftly, without knocking, he opened the door and slipped inside.

Jud Hawkins stared at him from where he sat in his bath.

It was a clumsy affair, that bath, thin iron painted and ornamented with flowers. The big man filled it to overflowing and little pools of water lay on the polished floor around him. He stared at Thorne, reached for a jug and rising, tipped the clean water over his head. Setting down the jug he picked up a towel, rubbed himself dry, then slipped on shirt and trousers. Habit made him strap his gun-belt around his waist.

'That's better,' he said. 'Travelling sure does make a man dirty.'

'Water can wash off more than dirt,' said Thorne. He looked at the big man. 'Eighteen ninety-four.'

'Twenty thirty-two.'

'All right,' said Thorne. 'I don't know you and you don't know me but the passwords are as they should be and I guess you're the man I want.' He stepped across to the door, locked it, and returned to the side of the big man.

'What kept you?'

'I ran into some trouble,' said Jud easily. 'I was jumped by a couple of drifters. They shot my horse and I had trouble picking up another!'

'And the drifters?'

Jud smiled and touched the gun at his waist.

'Just so as I know.' Thorne frowned. 'What was the idea of taking a bath?'

'Why not? The orders were that I should come to Springfield, order a room and bath, and then wait for someone to contact me. Seems pointless ordering a bath and not using it, suspicious too. Why?'

'It was out of character. The clerk got to wondering why a cowhand should want to take a bath.'

'That's what I thought,' agreed Jud. 'But you know what's behind it more than I do. The instructions were plain, I guess they were like that to avoid any chance of mistaken identity.' Jud stopped and finished dressing. He slipped on his coat, adjusted the butt of his pistol and eased the knife at his belt. 'All right, now what?'

'There's a big shipment of rifles leaving here at dawn. Ammunition too as well as troops for the front. It's imperative that the train be stopped, wrecked if you like, before it reaches its destination.'

'Do you know the route?'

'Yes.' Thorne fumbled in his pocket and drew out a scrap of paper. 'I've got it here. The best place to wreck the train would be at Murry's Bridge just after Twin Falls. A few sticks of dynamite will bring down the bridge and train both.'

'Maybe.' Jud reached out and took the paper. He stared at it, frowning at the faint lines. 'Open country until we hit the foothills. If the train keeps to schedule it will reach Twin Falls by sunset tomorrow. That means hard riding.'

'I know it.' Thorne took a cigar case from his pocket and selected a cigar. He

10

passed one to Jud, lit them, breathed smoke. 'You should have arrived yesterday. I was getting worried and getting ready to run. For all I knew you could have been captured and the truth screwed out of you.' His eyes narrowed behind a veil of smoke. 'In fact that very thing could have happened. How do I know that I can trust you?'

'You don't,' said Jud. 'Any more than I can trust you. For all either of us knows we could be setting our necks in a noose.' He smiled at the worried expression of the other man. 'Look, friend,' he said. 'I don't even know the name you're going under. Suppose you tell me?'

'Thorne. Blake Thorne from Montana Territory. Well?'

'You heard my name down at the desk.' Jud's smile widened. 'Yes, I spotted you hiding behind your paper. I collected your name too from Rastus, money seems to loosen plenty of tongues in Springfield. You're a trader and you move around quite a lot.

11

Popular with the officers and with the men too. They trust you, drink with you, and let you stab them in the back.'

'Is that the way you see it?'

'No, it's the way they would take it if they knew. The would call you a spy, Thorne, a dirty Reb spy, and they wouldn't let you die easy.'

'The same goes double for you, mister.' Thorne was angry, his sallow cheeks flushed dusty red. 'If I was to let on who and what you are they'd tie you to a couple of horses going in opposite directions. They'd do it Indian fashion. Quantrill's Raiders aren't what you'd call popular in this region.'

'So I ride with Quantrill,' said Jud. 'So what?'

'So that makes you a fair target for any soldier or civilian,' said Thorne. 'The soldier would do it because it's his duty to kill the enemy. The civilian would do it for fun and for the bounty money. If you ask me the game isn't worth it. If you want to fight then why not join the regulars? A suit of grey would protect you from being shot out of hand by the first suspicious, trigger-happy bounty-hunter. Where's the profit in what you do?'

'Where's the profit in any war?' Jud turned and stared out of the window. Below him, in the street, a column of fresh-faced soldiers marched towards the railhead, the sound of their boots echoing from the false-fronts of the houses and saloons, stores and hotels. Thorne joined him, his cigar glowing red against the window.

'It's getting late,' he said. 'Dawn tomorrow, don't forget that, it doesn't leave you much time.'

'No,' said Jud. He stared at the other man. 'You asked me what was in it for me, Thorne, well what's in it for you? Why do you act the spy and risk your neck?'

'Don't you know?'

'I'm asking you.'

'Why I do what I do is my business,' said Thorne slowly. 'I don't ask you questions, why ask me?' His eyes narrowed again. 'Talk like that makes me uneasy. Maybe I'd better ask you some questions, just to make sure that you are who you're supposed to be. Where is Quantrill now?'

'That's his business!'

'And mine. I'm in this thing as deep as you are. If he's going to blow up that bridge he must be somewhere near. Is he at Platt's Mills?'

'No.'

'Wayward's Fork?'

'No.'

'Fort Underwood?' Thorne shook his head. 'No, he wouldn't be there. Where is he?'

Jud didn't answer. Instead he stared at the other man with a peculiar intentness and, beneath that stare, Thorne flushed and looked nervous.

'Forget it,' he said. 'I guess I talked out of turn.'

'Maybe.' Jud thinned his lips. 'I saw a poster as I rode into town,' he said deliberately. 'Seems the bounty has risen quite a piece since I last saw one.

14

A smart man might think it a good idea to collect that money.'

'Would he?'

'But a really smart man would remember that it would be easier catching a rattlesnake with his bare hands than trying to corral Quantrill.'

'I said forget it.'

'Sure, but you set me thinking. Suppose that you aren't the man I was supposed to meet? Suppose that you're a Northern agent trying to trap Quantrill? Seems to me that a man like that would ask just the questions you've done.'

'I'm not sure of you either,' reminded Thorne. 'How can I be?'

'You can't.' Jud stared at the cigar between his fingers and then stared out of the window. Outside it was dark but not too dark for him to miss the shapes lurking in doorways, shapes which betrayed their presence by occasional glints of metal and patches of colour. The glints and patches to be expected from men wearing uniform.

He sighed, conscious of a tightening of his stomach, the unmistakable signs of danger. For a long moment he stood at the window, his mind busy with plans, and, when he turned, his face was impassive.

'I guess we're both living on our nerves,' he said easily. 'This sort of war isn't to my liking. I'd prefer to meet the enemy man to man, not skulking like a wolf ready to pounce.' He sighed again. 'Personally I'd be glad to see the whole thing over and done with.'

And in that he spoke nothing but the simple truth.

For almost four years now the North and South had been locked in civil combat and the fertile soil of the east was red with the blood of both sides. The Northern Union battled the Southern Confederacy in a struggle all the more bitter because it was brother against brother, ideal against ideal. The South, their backs to the wall, were literally fighting for their lives, desperately trying to hold back Sherman and his advancing armies. In order to do that anything and everything was acceptable to the Confederacy, even the band of adventurers gathered together by Quantrill.

Bold men they were who rode with Quantrill. Hard, fearless, ruthless and devoted to a cause which, in their hearts, they knew was hopeless. A band of guerrillas, uniformed, striking like a thrown knife at installations and military establishments deep in the supposed safety of the North, bringing fear and terror to the enemies of the South.

To the Southern Confederacy they were patriots, worth twenty times their number of regular troops, equipped and paid as far as possible from the war-chests of the Rebels. But Quantrill had claimed that, to be totally effective, his independent band must operate as far as it could without outside aid and, by taking what he needed from the enemy, he helped the South by that much more.

To the North they were brigands, outlaws, unprotected by the grey uniform of the South, by accepted military rank, by any of the usages and customs of war. If captured they would be hanged or shot without trial or hesitation. They carried a price on their heads and each member of the band trod the line between death and dubious safety.

Jud Hawkins was one of them.

He had ridden into Springfield on a desperate mission, risking discovery every step of the way. Strangers were always suspect, more so in this town which manufactured the famous Springfield rifle, forerunner of the Winchester, and was the assembly point of newly trained troops for the Northern Army.

'I know how you feel,' said Thorne after a pause. He gestured towards the window. 'Look at those kids out there, boys most of them, marching off to war as if to a great adventure. They are going to die fast enough without us helping them on the way. Isn't it enough that we should be at each other's throats without having to stoop to dirty fighting? It isn't war to wreck a train, it's murder. It's dirty. It's more like Indian fighting than the way white men settle their differences.' He stared at Jud. 'Don't you agree with me?'

'Maybe.'

'Don't you ever feel sick of riding with Quantrill?' said Thorne. 'I would if I were you. I'd try to get out of it and be clean again.' He looked at his cigar. 'You know, I reckon that if I had the chance I'd take an amnesty and make a fresh start.'

'Is the chance going?'

'Didn't you read the poster?'

'Only to glance at it!'

'If anyone wants to give themselves up the North will grant an amnesty for all past crimes.' Thorne stared at his cigar again. 'If such a person wanted to earn himself the bounty money by turning in Quantrill, then he could do that too.'

'Nice.' A muscle rippled high on

Jud's cheek. 'You aiming to collect that bounty?'

'Me?' Thorne shook his head. 'No. I just collect information and hand it over to one of Quantrill's men. That's all I do. What happens after that is no concern of mine.'

'That's right,' said Jud. He stared out of the window again. 'About that train, you say it carries guns and troops both?'

'Yes.'

'Leaving at dawn?'

'That's right.' Thorne gestured with his cigar. 'If you hope to catch it at Twin Falls you'd better get moving. You've got to contact Quantrill and get there before sunset tomorrow.'

'Yes,' said Jud. 'My horse is jaded so I'll have to get another. Can you help me?'

'Zeke down in the livery stables will fix you up.'

'Sure.' Jud hesitated. 'Anything else before I go?'

'No. Better have Quantrill send in a

man ten days from now. I'll have more information for him by that time.' Thorne smiled and stuck out his hand. 'Good luck, fellow. The quicker we win this war the better. Right?'

'Right.'

Jud smiled and shook the other man by the hand. He looked around the room, shook his head at the bath, and stepped towards the door. He moved softly, lithely, betraying a hidden strength in the way he moved. Thorne stared after him as he left the room then, sighing, stepped towards the window.

Below, in the street, the lurking shapes stiffened as Jud stepped from the hotel.

2

Jud paused as he entered the street, his eyes watchful as he glanced at the dimly seen shapes. Behind him the lights of the hotel cast a glow over the dusty boardwalk and other lights, from the saloons and stores, gave the street an unreal appearance. For a moment he stood, his shadow huge and sprawling before him then, with deceptive casualness, he sauntered towards the livery stable. Zeke, his wrinkled face creased in a grin, nodded to him as he slipped through the double doors.

'Come for your stuff?'

'Yes.' Jud handed the old man a cigar, lit it, then lit his own. 'How's the horse?'

'Beat, you won't be riding that mount for a few days.'

'No.' Jud drew on his cigar, his eyes searching the face of the old man. 'Can you let me have a horse, a good one?'

'Sure, you want one?'

'Yes.'

'Riding out right away?'

'That's the idea.'

Zeke nodded and stared with frank curiosity at the tall man. 'That horse of yours was all in,' he said slowly. 'You don't look any too spry yourself. Business urgent?'

'Could be.'

'Where are you heading?'

'Does it matter?' Jud tensed, aware of the soft creak of leather outside the doors. He grunted and, taking the old man by the arm, led him deeper into the stables. He paused between the stalls where horses nuzzled their feed. The place was rank with the smell of sweat and leather. Zeke looked up, his eyes shrewd in his weatherbeaten face.

'Trouble, stranger?'

'Did I say that?' Jud dug a handful of coins from his pocket. 'Pick me a horse, a good one, and take mine in part trade. Switch saddles and the rest of my gear.'

'I've a mare, she had a sprained fetlock but she's fit now.' Zeke paused by a stall. 'I won her off an officer in a poker game. I guess that we can make a deal.'

Jud nodded, his eyes thoughtful as the old man took his saddle and threw it across the mare. She whinnied, pawing the ground as, if eager to be on the move. Jud stepped forward, checked the cinch strap, adjusted the saddlebags and loosened the rifle in its scabbard. He bent and let his fingers run over the slender legs of the horse.

'How much?'

'Fifty dollars and call it even!' Zeke licked his lips. 'Horse-flesh comes expensive in these parts, but she's a good horse.'

'I'm not arguing.' Jud counted the coins in his hand, shrugged, replaced them and took out a wad of greenbacks. He peeled off fifty dollars, paused, peeled off ten more, and gave the notes to the old man. 'You got a back way out of here, Zeke?'

'Sure.'

'I'd like to use it.' He smiled at the other's expression. 'As a favour from one Texas man to another.'

'So you're from Texas? I guessed so,' Zeke chuckled. 'Know Houston? Dallas? Austin?'

'I've passed through them,' admitted Jud. 'I was raised in Fort Worth myself.'

'You don't say!' Zeke grinned even wider. 'I know that part well. My Pa was a trader operating from the Fort. He lost his hair to the Apaches.'

'Those Indians are sure the devil,' said Jud. He took hold of the horse's reins. 'Say, you know the country around here, what's the quickest way to get to Plattes Falls?'

'Head due south after passing the railhead,' said the old man promptly. 'You'll make it by dawn or sooner. It ain't a hard ride and the trail is plain.' He stared at Jud. 'Is that where you're heading?'

'Maybe, why?'

'If you are then you can call in at Burke's Tavern about fifteen miles out of town. He brews a mean punch and can fix up the horse. Might do to rest a while if you feel tuckered.'

'I'll remember that,' said Jud. He stared at the old man. 'How about showing me that back way?'

'Sure.' Zeke moved dawn between the stalls and pushed open a door. A narrow passage lay beyond, the end illuminated with light from the houses. A mounted man sat his horse and stared at nothing. His silhouette blocked the end of the passage and, at the light from the stables, he turned, one hand falling to his side. His horse snickered and pawed the dust.

Jud reached out and shut the door. He turned the mare and led it towards the front entry. His lips had thinned to a mere gash and his eyes had grown hard and stony in the grim planes of his face. Zeke stared at him, saying nothing, then shrugged and ran forward. Jud mounted, loosened the pistol at his belt, and nodded to the old man.

'Open her up, old-timer.'

'Sure.' Zeke swung wide the double doors and Jud rode out into the street.

He wasn't alone. He could tell it even though he rode like a man sunk deep in thought, guiding his horse with his knees rather than the reins. The mare was skittish, inclined to prance and eager to step out. He restrained her, his eyes flickering from side to side beneath the shadow of his hat. Men drifted in the same direction as himself, mounted men, wearing, civilian clothing but with a certain unmistakable stiffness about them. All were armed.

Jud sighed and reached for a cigar. He lit it, throwing the flaring match into the dust and guided his horse towards the edge of town. A small body of riders passed him, spurring down the street as if intent on their mission. The railhead came into view, brilliantly lit by flaring lamps, the hissing of steam filling the air with sibilance. Troops thronged the station, armed and watchful and beyond them the long rows of cars and wagons rested on the shining rails. An engine, sparks flying from the smoke-box, chugged and hissed as it shunted wagons from the warehouses.

Jud passed the railhead, swung due south, and let his horse break into a canter. The lights of town fell away behind him and, aside from the faint light of the stars, he rode in darkness. Before him the trail unwound like a dirty length of cotton, rutted and visible only as a lighter streak between two masses of darkness. The sound of the mare's hoofs drummed on the parched dirt as she lengthened her stride.

Jud rode for maybe a couple of miles and then, without letting the mare break step, he swung from the saddle, kicked his feet free of the stirrups, hung for a moment by the saddle horn, then dropped, bringing his hand hard against the mare's rump as he did so. Immediately the horse broke into a gallop and Jud, rolling from his fall, buried himself in the sage at the side of the trail, his eyes staring back towards town.

He did not have to wait long. A party of men, about a dozen of them, came spurring down the trail, the sounds of their mounts loud in the silence. They passed with a creak of leather and a jingle of spurs and, as they passed, one man rose in his saddle, his hand upraised for silence. They drew rein, sitting like statues in the dim starlight and, through the night, the sound of the galloping mare echoed with startling clarity.

'He's opened up,' said one of the riders. 'Shall we catch him, Sarge?'

'We trail him.' The leader gestured and the party rode off down the trail. In the sage, hidden from any casual glance, Jud grinned and, after a while, rose and began walking back to town.

It was a long walk for a man wearing riding boots and he was tired from his previous exertions. By the time the lights of town had grown near Jud felt as if he would have given his soul for a bottle of whiskey, a meal, and a warm bed. He dismissed the notion, standing well beyond the area of light around the railhead, his eyes narrowed as he watched the sentries. An engine fussed up and down the track, going to beyond the circle of light and returning with a hiss of steam as it shunted the cars and wagons up to and beyond the warehouses. At the limit of its run a cloud of steam from the boiler drifted like thick mist over the tracks before it dissipated into the night. Jud stared at it, gauging distances with his eye then, moving like a shadow, drifted through the darkness towards the edge of the area of light where the gleaming rails lost themselves in the night.

A sentry patrolled the line but he was easily avoided and Jud, waiting his chance, dived across the rails and dropped between them just as a cloud of steam billowed around him, shielding him from view. He grunted, blinked his eyes, then grabbed frantically at the back of the engine tender as the engine started forward. The lights brightened around him and he cowered even lower, riding the tender scant inches above the rails, almost strangling in the scalding rush of steam surging around him. The engine slowed, struck, pushed and the wheels spun a moment before gripping. Jud peered around the edge of the tender, waited until the engine had drawn level with the line of cars and then, just before it backed again, dropped, rolled, and dived frantically between the wheels of the motionless train.

He hugged the cinders, watchful, waiting for one of the sentries to shout a challenge. None did, his manoeuvre, crude though it had been, had proved a success.

Near the train, a few yards distant, the bulk of a warehouse loomed huge and foreboding. Sentries patrolled it, their paths crossing and recrossing as they marched, their carbines on their shoulders, their boots heavy against the cindery soil. From his position beneath the train Jud watched them guessing from the men's vigilance that the warehouse contained something both valuable and important. He turned, staring down the train, then looked back at the warehouse. The end of the line of wagons was some distance away and, as he calculated time and distance, Jud nodded.

Cautiously he began to work his way between the wheels, hugging the cinders between the rails and freezing whenever anyone came too close. Reaching the end of the train he unbuttoned his shirt, reached inside it and brought forth a small package. Unwrapping it he disclosed two sticks of dynamite and a length of fuse. He stared upwards at the bottom of the wagon beneath which he crouched, then back at the warehouse. He nodded, took his knife from his belt, cut off about a quarter of one of the sticks, fastened a detonator to it and measured off a length of fuse. The remaining dynamite he tied in a bundle, fixed a second detonator, coupled a short length of fuse and tucked it into his jacket pocket.

The smaller bomb he tied beneath the wagon, lashing it firmly with a length of rawhide against the wooden flooring. He checked the detonator, re-measured the fuse, tested the lashing, then fumbled in his pockets for cigarette makings and a match. He rolled a cigarette with steady fingers, put it between his lips, crouched low and struck a match, shielding the flare with his hands and body. He lit the cigarette, drew it to ruby life, killed the match and then, after a careful look around, touched the glowing end of the cigarette to the fuse of the bomb.

Hesitating only long enough to be sure that it had caught he turned and made his way as fast as he could down the train, crouching between the wheels and mentally counting off the seconds as he moved. He arrived opposite the warehouse, removed the other bomb from his pocket, drew on his cigarette and then, when he had reached the end of his count, dived forward between the wheels and away from the train.

A sentry saw him, stared, shouted a challenge and grabbed at his carbine. Jud rolled, tasting cinders as a bullet dug into the ground inches from his face, then he felt the structure of the warehouse dig into his side. He rose, dived for the shelter of the building, and dropped down just as the entire end of the train exploded with a gush of flame and roaring fury.

For a second following the explosion everything seemed to be frozen, standing still as if numbed by the shocking violence of the man-made thunder. A great blossom of flame reached up from the line of wagons, and pieces of flaming wood showered sparks as they lanced through the night. Even they seemed to move in slow motion so that, to the shocked sentries, they turned and fell as if figments from a dream. They stared, wondering and shocked, then, following their instincts, ran towards the burning men and the screams of the injured.

All but Jud.

Even as the dynamite had exploded he was on the move. Waiting only long enough for the blast to expend itself, he rose, dived around the corner towards the doors of the warehouse, and thrust himself against them. They were locked, fastened by a great padlock and staple, and they resisted his thrust as if they were part of a mountain. Without pause he snatched the Colt from his belt and blasted three shots at the padlock, thumbing the hammer so that the three explosions rolled and merged into one. Metal yielded before the hammer blows of the bullets and, when he thrust a second time against the doors, they gaped to reveal rows and stacks of boxes each stencilled with the military markings of the Union Forces.

Even before Jud had seen the boxes he was in a flurry of smooth action. He lifted the bomb to his lips, touched his cigarette to the short fuse, threw the bomb into the warehouse and was running towards the sheltering darkness before the first soldier had heard the shots, recognized them, turned, seen the invader and had lifted his carbine.

Jud felt lead whine across his shoulder, twisted, ducked, then, as he mentally counted, threw himself desperately on the gritty soil.

Behind him all hell opened in a gushing tower of noise and smoke and flaming destruction. It was almost too loud for reality, a thundering wave of roaring sound which, instead of dying, doubled itself and then doubled itself again into a rolling, blasting, searing wave of destruction. The roof of the warehouse lifted in a thousand burning fragments, lifted on a pillar of eyescaring brilliance. Noise and blast rolled in every direction, flattening, killing, destroying. The train, heavy as it was, tilted and rolled as if made of cardboard, the tracks buckled, an engine blasted out and abruptly disintegrated and, with the roar of the explosion, the sounds of injured men screaming for assistance died in the greater calamity.

Died only to return in greater force when the echoes had faded into something nearer silence.

Jud didn't wait for that. He felt the blast tug at him, cringed as the air became full of whining death, and felt his skin crackle as something hot and burning fell on his leg. He beat out the flames and, the leg of his trousers still smouldering, lunged further away from the burning warehouse. He bumped smack against a wild-eyed sentry.

The man was in rags, a thick stream of blood running down his face from a lacerated scalp, and had lost his carbine. He clutched at Jud, the light from the flames making his eyes glisten like those of an animal.

'What happened?' he said. 'What set it off?' He flinched as a dull thunder shook the flaming building. 'I'm getting out of here! That place is stuffed with ammunition.'

Jud watched him go, running, looking back over his shoulder, staggering and swaying as if he were drunk. Fresh explosions shook the air and Jud dropped as something droned overhead. Before him the soldier screamed, spun and fell. As he toppled he clutched at his stomach and Jud could see where the blood spurted from a ghastly wound. Tight-lipped, he stared back at the building. It still flung sparks high to the sky and, from time to time, the sharp, ripping detonations of exploding cartridges filled the air with noise and hot lead. The wild bullets, set off by the heat, were proving more dangerous than the actual initial explosion itself.

Men began to run towards the warehouse, uniformed, armed, led by officers shouting harsh commands.

'Sergeant. Take a patrol and cover the tracks. Stop anyone you meet and I mean stop them. Shoot to kill if necessary.'

'Yes, sir.'

'You spread your men around the perimeter. Keep low, there may be more explosions, but I don't want a mouse to get past you.'

'Yes, sir.' A second party of men hurried away to obey the commands. Jud, watching them, felt the familiar tightening of his stomach. His plan had depended on speed and audacity. It had worked — up to a point, but now he had to make good his own escape. As he crept forward he cursed the blind luck which had made his target an ammunition store. The hail of bullets had pinned him down long enough for the troops to get organized.

He rose and staggered forward, swaying and acting as though injured. A sentry challenged him, the firelight rippling on the cold steel of his bayonet, and the same firelight reflecting from his eyes gave him a peculiarly inhuman look. Jud halted, swayed, staggered a few steps forward, then crashed on his face.

'Get up!' The sentry stared down at

Jud, undecided as to what to do. If the man were an innocent victim then he was entitled to good care and treatment, but the sentry had had his orders and they were plain. Stop everyone in the area. He reached forward and prodded with the point of his bayonet.

'You heard me! On your feet!'

'Can't.' Jud thrashed, made as if to rise, then slumped back to the dirt. Again the bayonet prodded and this time, when he rose, Jud did it in one swift, flowing motion. His left arm knocked aside the rifle, his right fist swung in a short arc and connected with the sentry's jaw. The soldier dropped without a sound.

Swiftly Jud made his way towards the centre of town, away from the railhead and the shouts and screams of disorganised and injured men.

The town was wide awake and as curious as only a town can be. Men thronged the dusty streets asking questions and finding their own answers. Jud weaved among them, avoiding those who wanted to question him, and finally made his way towards the edge of town. He halted close to a saloon, a place catering for the transients, cowhands and settlers fringing Springfield. Some horses stood hitched to the rail, saddled and ready to go, stamping and pawing the ground as they waited for their masters who were either drinking inside or, more likely, had left the saloon to see what all the noise was about. Jud stood in a doorway, measuring the horses with his eyes then, stepping boldly forward, walked directly to a big grey and unhitched it from the rail. He was putting his foot in the stirrup when a man called to him from the doorway of the saloon.

'That you, Fred?'

Jud grunted something, bending down as if to tighten the cinch strap.

'Going back so soon?' The man stepped down from the boardwalk and came towards the horses. 'Did you hear all the noise? Sounded like as if the arsenal went up. Some bang.' From the sound of his voice it was obvious that he had been drinking and was more amused by the fuss than anything else.

'I guess one of those soldier boys must have dropped a match or something. What do you say, Fred?'

Again Jud grunted, fuming at the bad luck which had brought this fellow on to the boardwalk at just the wrong time.

'What's the matter, Fred?' The man came nearer. 'I know you're there because I saw you unhitch your horse. Playing hard to get?' He chuckled again. 'Say. Fred, I . . . '

'Stow it!' Jud stepped towards the man, his Colt levelled in his hand. 'Stow it and you won't get hurt!'

'You ain't Fred!' The man blinked whiskey-bleared eyes. 'You was stealing his horse. You lousy horsethief. You know what we do with scum like you?'

'Stow it.' Jud rammed the nose of his pistol against the other's chest. 'Button your lip or I'll open you up.'

'You don't scare me,' snapped the

man. 'A horsethief is a yellow-bellied rattlesnake and I aim to prove it!' He opened his mouth, half-turned as if to shout towards the saloon, then stiffened as Jud brought the barrel of his pistol against his skull.

'Sorry.' Jud holstered his gun and caught the man as he fell. 'Personally I agree with you, a horse-thief should be strung up and left to dry, but this ain't no time for it.'

He dragged the man to the side of the street, returned to the grey, mounted and spurred towards the open country beyond town. He rode due west, cutting directly across the sage, and after a while began to swing to the south. Once he halted and glanced back, narrowing his eyes as he stared into the starlit darkness. Far away, low on the horizon, the red flames of the burning warehouse still threw sparks into the air, glowing like a swarm of angry bees as they leaped and spun, twinkled and darted before fading to vanish in the silent darkness.

Jud stared at them for a long time, his ears alert for sound of possible pursuit then, satisfied that no one trailed him, he dug spurs into the flanks of his stolen horse and rode towards the south.

Towards Quantrill.

3

General John McKenzie sat at his desk and stared at the reports before him. He was a tall, thin, round-shouldered man whose hair had long since lost its original colour and was now as white as the snow which capped the mountains to the north. He wore his uniform with the easy grace of a man to whom civilian garments were strange. He wore a row of ribbons on his left chest. His pistol holster was carried well to the front. His left sleeve was pinned back, the empty material swinging a little as he moved. He looked up as the door opened and a young man dressed also in the blue of the Union entered the office.

'You sent for me, sir?'

'Yes.' The general nodded to the orderly and, when the man had gone, gestured to a chair. 'Sit down, Captain. Smoke?'

'Thank you, sir.'

'Try these.' McKenzie pushed a box of cigars across his desk. 'Real Virginian. We found them in a wagon and took charge of them as contraband.' A wintry smile touched the corners of his mouth. The captain answered it, well knowing what the older man meant. He relaxed, drawing at his cigar.

'Captain Sam Wayland,' said the general and rolled the name around his tongue as if he liked the taste. 'Young, unmarried, born in the South and trained at West Point. Gained promotion in the field of battle, twice wounded, taken prisoner but escaped, noted for outstanding heroism. A fine record, Captain.'

'Thank you, sir.'

'Do you know why I sent for you, Captain?'

'No, sir.'

'Not even a guess?'

'I've learned that guessing, in the army, is a waste of time,' smiled Sam. 'Either you know, or you reserve judgment. Guesswork can lead you into a lot of grief.'

'A wise philosophy,' said the old man. 'Still, if you haven't made a guess then the army isn't what it was in my young days.' He sighed. 'Not that that is the only difference. This goldarn war . . . ' He broke off and helped himself to a cigar. 'You know what happened last night?'

'Yes, sir,' said Sam grimly. 'I was on duty. A train wrecked and an entire warehouse of ammunition blown sky-high.'

'Twenty men dead, fifty injured and the railhead thrown into utter confusion,' added the general. He puffed smoke and stared at the tip of his cigar. 'Start guessing, Captain. What caused it?'

'I don't have to guess,' said Sam. 'I told you that I was on duty. I was in the guard-house when the first bang went off and on my way out when the second came. If it hadn't been for the wild bullets filling the air I'd have been on the scene quicker than I was. But as things were we had to take cover until it was safe to move.'

'I'm not blaming you, Captain, you did well.' The general puffed more smoke. 'Accident?'

'No.' Thin lines of anger deepened from nose to mouth as the captain threw aside the suggestion. 'That was no accident.'

'Guessing, Captain?'

'Dynamite, General. I've heard giant powder go off before and can recognize it when I hear it. I'd say that there were two separate detonations.'

'And you'd be right.' McKenzie straightened in his chair. 'That warehouse was sabotaged, bombed with dynamite, and our war effort hindered by the loss of ammunition, men, transportation and other material.' He waved the cigar. 'But you know all about that. That isn't why I sent for you.'

'No, sir?'

'No.'

McKenzie fell silent, his eyes on the papers before him. Sam, sitting smoking in the chair, wondered what all this was about. He felt tired, he had been up all night helping to organise the rescue parties, and his eyelids felt heavy in the warm, close air of the office. He jerked to full awareness as the old man began to speak again.

'What do you know of Quantrill, Captain?'

'Quantrill?'

'Yes, surely you've heard of him?'

Sam nodded. 'I have, and nothing to his credit.' He frowned. 'Where does he come in?'

'I'll give you the full picture,' said McKenzie as if arriving at a sudden decision. 'We have known for some time that information about movements of troops and supplies from Springfield has been reaching the enemy. We didn't know just how until recently, but we did know that we have lost too many men and too much material to the raiders for it to have been coincidence.

Obviously, someone in Springfield was in contact with Quantrill. To make it short, we found him.'

'A soldier?'

'No, a civilian. A trader by the name of Thorne.' McKenzie sighed. 'We caught him, threatened him, and he refused to speak. However, among his effects we found some papers, among them a date, a name, and a number. Knowing what we did we took a chance. In other words we planted our own agent to contact Quantrill's man.'

'I see.' Sam became even more awake, this was getting interesting. 'When did he arrive?'

'Yesterday.'

'But . . . ?' Sam blinked. 'No, no it must have been sheer bad luck. You caught him, of course.'

'No.'

'You mean he escaped or didn't he turn up?'

'He turned up. Our man contacted him, he rode off and the next thing we knew was the railhead exploding all over the place!' McKenzie shrugged at the young man's expression. 'So we took a chance and it failed. I still think it was worth it.'

'Twenty men dead, General? Fifty injured?'

'This is war, Captain. Civil war, the worst kind there is!' McKenzie swallowed and regained his calm. 'Let me give you the facts. Our agent contacted Quantrill's man and, as far as he knew, everything went according to plan. He passed over the information, discovered that the raider was riding off right away, and let him go. Other men followed him and, if he hadn't somehow become suspicious, he would have led us direct to Quantrill and his gang of cut-throats. But he did become suspicious. He gave our men the slip and, as far as I can gather, he doubled back, bombed the railhead, then stole a horse and made his escape.'

'Yes, General.'

'I took a chance, Captain,' said McKenzie tightly. 'I had no idea that anything would happen to the railhead and I still can't see just how it was worked. But never mind that, the main thing is that I considered it worth risking the raider escaping on the gamble that he would guide us to his leader. I lost the gamble. Quantrill knows that we are suspicious of him here and he will not give us another chance. The problem now is to save something from the mess.' He leaned forward. 'That's where you come in.'

'Me?'

'You, Captain.'

Sam blinked and looked at his superior officer.

'I'm not going silly in my old age, Captain,' gritted McKenzie. 'This is what I propose. I want you to take leave of absence and go and find Quantrill. Will you accept the assignment?'

For a moment the young man was tempted to laugh and then, remembering the other's rank, he coughed instead. The cough dragged on as the ludicrousness of what the other had suggested struck home and he was almost choking before he managed to retain a straight face.

'Laugh, if you want to, Captain,' said McKenzie coldly. 'Laugh out loud and get it over with then, maybe, you can pay some attention to what I'm going to say.'

'Yes, sir.' Sam sobered and felt a little ashamed as the old man stared at him. 'I'm sorry, sir.'

'I know why you feel like laughing,' said the old man. 'In a way I don't blame you but this isn't the time for laughter. You think that the idea of going out and finding Quantrill is one of the most stupid concepts you've ever heard. Am I right?'

'The entire army has been looking for him, sir,' reminded Sam. 'If they can't catch him how can one man?'

'I'll come to that later. Just at this moment I want to rid your mind of any false notions concerning Quantrill. He isn't just a brigand, you know, not just another opportunist thrown up by the

53

war. He is dangerous, last night proves that, and he must be stopped at all costs. I can tell you that he has done more to hurt the North than any two regiments. He strikes deep in the heart of our possessions, destroys, kills, then rides away back to the safety of the South. Naturally an army can't find him. Naturally they can't catch him. But what an army can't do, one man might.' He stared at Sam. 'If that man joined up with him and later betrayed him.'

'I am a soldier, sir,' said Sam, stiffly. 'Not a spy.'

'Am I asking you to be a spy?' McKenzie snorted, puffed at his cigar, swore when he discovered that it had died on him, and re-lit it. 'I put it in its worst form so as not to deceive you, but don't let's haggle over words. Quantrill does not stick to the rules of war. He fights without uniform and so is liable to be shot as a spy at any time. To fight him we too must forget the rules. To get a man into his band, one of our men, is the only hope we have of destroying him. I don't mean that he will go on for ever as he is, but I do mean that we must smash him before he has a chance to do us any more stupid, senseless, killing damage.'

'Senseless, sir?'

'That's what I said, Captain. At this very moment our forces are moving towards Gettysburg. If Sherman can smash the Confederate Army then his way will be open to the sea. Once he gets the Rebs on the run the war will be over aside from the shouting. In other words, Captain, we've got the best chance of ending this insane conflict now than at any time during the past four years. I don't want anything happening to spoil it.'

'As close as that?' Sam felt warm as he thought about it. He had seen too much of war to have any stupid notions as to it being romantic or glorious. He remembered the stench of the dead, the field hospitals, the screams of the boys as they saw the enemy, their own people, coming to kill them. It would be better when the war was over, far better than training one half of the nation to kill the other.

McKenzie knocked the ash from his cigar.

'It is very important that we crush Quantrill, Captain. Leave it at that and never mind the whys and wherefores. Think of last night and you will have your answer. Now I want yours, will you do it?'

'Are you asking me to volunteer, sir?'

'Yes.'

'I . . . ' Sam hesitated, the more he thought about the scheme the more insane it became. McKenzie stared at him, his old eyes shrewd and, as Sam fumbled for words, brought his remaining hand down on the desk with a bang.

'Hold it, Captain!' He picked up his cigar and puffed it to fresh life. 'I must be getting old. Of course you can't see the sense in it and I've no right asking you to volunteer for a mission without knowing what it's all about.' He smiled, then, lifting his voice, yelled an order to his orderly.

'Bring Slade in here.'

He waited until the man had joined them, made the introductions, then settled back.

'Slade, this is the man who may try to finish what we started. Tell him about the man you saw.'

'Quantrill's man?'

'That's the one.'

'Well,' said Slade, 'there isn't much to tell really. He registered as we knew he would, false name obviously, and gave me the password. I told him the train movements we had fixed up and we chatted some before he left.'

'Anything about him struck you as unusual?' Sam leaned forward, interested for the first time. Slade rubbed his chin.

'He was no ignorant cowpuncher,' he said. 'He spoke like an educated man and had educated ideas. More like an officer, if you get me, gentle like and he used big words.'

'Anything else?'

'He didn't seem to like the war. We spoke about it and I went as far as I dared in trying to pump him. He didn't act as if he was suspicious, more tired than anything else, and he struck me as a man who was doing something he didn't really want to do but felt he had to do it.'

'I know what you mean,' said Sam. He looked at the general. 'Would it be possible for Quantrill to have Confederate army officers in his bunch?'

'Possibly, but unlikely. If he did they would have been with him from the first. As far as we know his latest recruits have been outlaws and wild men from the South and West.'

Sam nodded and stared at Slade. 'Anything else you noticed? What did he look like, what was he wearing, where did he seem to come from?'

'He was big,' said Slade. He eyed Sam. 'As tall as you, though a little broader in the shoulders. He moved slow and easy like a man who has lived in the open and who knows how to hunt or fight Indians. He carried his six-gun as though he knew how to use it.' Slade shrugged. 'Not much else to tell, I guess. He had deep set blue eyes, sunburned face, a thin mouth and a muscle twitched on one cheek when he was excited. I'd say he came from Texas, but I'm only guessing.'

'Zeke says the same,' put in the general. 'He says the stranger told him he was from Texas and they chatted about it. Zeke is pretty positive that's where he was born.' He nodded to Slade. 'That's all.'

Alone he stared at Sam. 'Well?'

'Not much to go on,' said Sam. 'But I can see why you picked me. I was born in Texas.'

'You're partly right,' admitted the general, 'you've the talk and walk, and you have the look of a Texas man. If you can drop your military bearing you'd pass for a Southerner.' He hesitated. 'Will you agree to the assignment?'

'I'll go, but can you give me more information?'

'What do you need?'

'Some idea as to where Quantrill hangs out. Some of the places I'd be likely to bump into some of his men. Anything like that.' Sam smiled. 'The South is a big place, General. I may go wandering for months before I strike it lucky if at all.'

'The only one who could have helped us was Thorne,' said McKenzie. 'I told you that we caught him. What I didn't tell you was that he made a fight for it. We shot it out with him and he died a few hours afterwards. We emptied his pockets but he wouldn't talk. He was in delirium towards the end and mentioned a name: Ranthorne. He repeated it often. Ever heard of it?'

'Ranthorne?' Sam frowned. 'Sounds like his own name. Could it be a ranch or something like that? A homesteading, maybe?'

'It could be,' admitted McKenzie. 'It isn't on any of the maps. He could have taken his name from a place, or named the place after himself, either way doesn't help us.' He leaned towards the young man. 'There it is, Captain. A name, a description, and an order. You take off your uniform, forget that you're a captain, and ride South to join Quantrill. You'll find him, join him, then ruin him and all his riders. You do all this under the threat of immediate death if discovered. It isn't a pretty task but it is an essential one if this nation is ever going to know full peace once more. Will you do it?'

'I'll try,' said Sam. He looked at the dead cigar between his fingers. 'It's a tall order for one man. Will I have any help?'

'Yes. I'll second Captain Leman to you, he knows the country and will act as your liaison. Anything else you need?'

'I don't think so.' He smiled as he thought about it. 'I've got the glimmering of a plan which might, just might turn out to be workable. I'll have to do things you may not like and . . . '

'Don't tell me.' McKenzie leaned forward, his face serious. 'I don't care what you do, Captain, or how you do it. I'm interested only in one thing. Get Quantrill! Get him dead or alive but get him. Do I make myself clear?'

'Yes, sir.'

'Then get on the job, Captain.' McKenzie stood up and stretched out his hand. 'Forget the war. Forget everything but the job in hand. Get Quantrill!'

4

From the top of the hill Jud Hawkins could see for miles in every direction, the rolling hills covered with trees and scrub looking fresh and new beneath the morning sun. He stood, his eyes searching the distance, probing the small patches of mist which still lingered in the hollows, running along the thin, thread-like trails which wound their way down into the valleys, over the hills, to vanish into mist and distance.

Behind him his horse whinnied and pawed the ground, the sound seeming to bring the big man back to a sense of reality. He sighed, shook himself and after a last, careful glance around, returned to his horse and the camp where he had spent the night.

The fire had died and he stooped, whittling thin slivers from a dry branch, heaping a little dried grass beneath them and touching them to flame. Thicker twigs fed the fire, followed by a few broken branches and soon, the blaze rose strong and smokeless into the still air. Filling his billy from a canteen Jud set it over the fire to boil. From his pack he took some meal, salt, a piece of bacon and a hunk of corn bread. He sliced a couple of thick rashers from the bacon, wet them, dipped them in the meal and suspended them on a green twig close to the fire. While his meal was cooking he shook out his blankets, rolled his pack and saddled the horse. It whinnied again, stretching out its nuzzle and he patted it, speaking soft and gentle as he soothed the restless beast.

The water boiling he threw in a handful of ground coffee, cut off a piece of the bread, took his barely cooked bacon from the twig and, sitting cross legged, ate and drank in thoughtful concentration. The meal over he rolled a cigarette, lit it, inhaled and returned to the brow of the hill for a further scrutiny of the countryside.

The hills were coming to life. From the distance he heard the sound of thin barking, the deeper voice of a man calling to the dogs, and the sharp, incredibly clear sound of an axe. A coach, the driver nodding on his box, the horses steaming in the chill morning air, came lumbering down the trail, disappearing beneath the trees only to reappear again smaller than it had before. Despite the sounds of life and waking activity the watcher could see no one and, satisfied, he returned to the fire, stamped it out, swung into his saddle and moved down the hill.

He rode all that morning, stopping at noon to feed and water the horse, chewing on a scrap of the corn bread as he waited for the animal to finish its feeding. Towards sunset the country changed, the rolling hills became harsher, more rugged, and the thick vegetation yielded to sparse sage, juniper and scrub. An hour before sundown Jud halted on a bluff, dropped from his horse, collected some sage and juniper leaves, built a fire and, when it was burning strong, threw on a handful of green leaves.

From his pack he took his blanket, spread it over the rising column of smoke, held it, then twisted it aside. A gush of thick smoke rose into the still air, to be followed by another, a third, then the smoke rose in an uninterrupted stream. A second time Jud sent up the three puffs of smoke and, after waiting a few minutes, repeated the signal. Replacing his blanket he extinguished the fire, mounted the horse and rode towards where a pair of jagged peaks rose from the foothills.

He entered the gulley between them, sent his mount up a narrow trail, and was glancing about with a worried expression when a man, almost invisible against the rock on which he lay, rapped a sharp challenge.

'Hold it! Keep your hands high, stranger. Move and I'll kill you.'

'Easy, Jonathan,' said Jud. 'Don't you know me?'

'Jud!' The man rose and came forward, his rifle in his hands. 'Man, it's sure good to see you.'

'Did you see my smoke?'

'Bart did. He spotted it and said that someone was heading this way. I didn't know that it was you, Jud.' He chuckled. 'Did I scare you?'

'Yes, but not in the way you think. You the outer guard?'

'That's right.'

'You're too far in. I could have planted an entire patrol in these hills before you could have seen me. Better move out a piece where you can see the approach.'

'Yes, Jud.' The man hesitated. 'Any news?'

'Some. How are things here?'

'As usual. We've been busy. Quantrill's back and waiting for you. Better not keep him dangling.'

Jud nodded and touched spurs to his mount. He rode for another mile, following a winding, almost invisible path, then suddenly came out on to a small clearing buried in the heart of the twin peaks. A few cabins rested against the rock, a staked corral, a cook shack and a smithy. The smith was working, the sound of his hammer made little ringing echoes from the rocks around and, as Jud moved forward, he heard the sharp hiss of iron being plunged into water.

Jud halted at the corral, stripped the saddle from his mount and sent it in to join the other horses. It snorted, kicked, then plunged forward, nosing the strangers and snickering as if in horse-talk. Jud humped his saddle, crossed to one of the cabins, kicked open the door and entered. It was empty but for items of personal nature scattered around. Little things mostly, a water-colour, a pair of rusty spurs, shaving mirrors, and old razor strops. A broken cartridge belt lay on one of the bunks and a couple of spent cartridge cases lay against the wall, shining golden in the last rays of the sun.

Jud tossed his saddle on to a bunk, unstrapped his bed-roll, took out razor, soap and towel and, leaving the cabin, went across to the wash-house. He washed, stripping off his shirt and laving his torso, shaved, dried himself and took his things back to the cabin. As he came out of the shack, a man, carrying a huge pail of water for the horses, stared at him and shouted a greeting.

'Jud! When did you get back?'

'Just now. Where are the others?'

'Most of them are out with Brenhardt. Quantrill is here, in his cabin, and the rest are asleep in the other cabins.' The man shifted his bucket. 'Any news?'

'Tell you later.'

'At chow?'

'Maybe.' Jud stared up at the sky. The sun had set and the tips of the twin peaks were painted with pink and gold, orange and amber. High above a wisp of cloud drifted, almost transparent against the darkening blue. The man tipped the bucket of water into the water trough, came to Jud, set down the bucket and fumbled in his pockets.

'Would you have the makings. Jud?'

'Try one of these.' Jud handed the man a handful of cigars.

'Thanks.' The man lit one, screwing up his eyes against the flare of the match. He was an old man, wrinkled, his skin more like leather than anything else. He limped a little as he walked. He breathed smoke and stared up at the sky.

'Purty, ain't it? Reminds me of the time when I was trapping up north. Must be more than thirty years ago now, nearer forty at a guess. Them was the times when a man could go up the Mississippi, right up to the Missouri, past the Three Forks and into Blackfoot country. The beaver was as thick as fleas on a hound dog, elk, goats, buffalo too.' He chuckled as he thought about it. 'I was a youngster then, not more than twenty, and I had me a real good Kentucky rifle. I sure earned a passel of money trapping beaver. I sure did.'

'I can imagine,' said Jud. He lit one of the cigars, feeling a strange reluctance to move, to break the spell of the dying day. He was tired, both mentally and physically, and the old man's words rippled like a stream over rocks, soothing and murmuring, the words losing themselves in the thickening twilight.

'Them was great days,' said the old man, and the red glow of his cigar turned his wrinkled face into something older than time itself. 'Trappers came from all over to trade their furs to the Company. We used to get maybe two, three dollars a time and spent it all on whiskey. Whiskey, traps, powder, ball, vermilion and trinkets for the Indians.' He sighed. 'We sure had ourselves a time.'

Jud nodded, not speaking.

'It was new country then,' continued the old man, speaking more to himself than to Jud. 'Big and wide and as clean as God made it. Indians owned it and the buffalo, elk and deer and beaver. A man could leave St Louis and head up river for as long as he could travel. He'd trap and hunt and winter with some of the Indians. The friendly Indians, that is, the Manadans, the Rees, Itoes or Crees. Not the Crow or Blackfoot, they'd take your hair as soon as look at you. Those were sure mean Indians.'

'Ever thought of going back?'

'Many times, but what's the use? The country ain't the same no more. The big river boats go upriver and the forts and settlements line it on both sides. The Indians are gone, or the few that are left spend their time begging whiskey and tobacco, and the game ain't what it used to be. Too many people up there now. They've trapped out the beaver and shot the game. Killing for fur and hide instead of meat and these new rifles didn't help any. With the old flintlocks a man had to have a sharp eye to hit his game and he couldn't shoot too often. Then the cap and ball guns came in and made it easier. Then the cartridge guns arrived, the Wessons, Sharps, Springfields and Henrys. Shooting game became something a blind man could do.' The old man sighed again. 'I sure do miss them days.'

'Yes,' said Jud. 'I know what you mean.'

'Maybe.' The old man sounded as though he didn't believe it. 'But you're too young to remember. I tell you that a man could ride for a week, a month even, and never set eye on a house, settlement or white man. He could find Indians if he wanted to but mostly he didn't. He was alone, all alone in a country so big that it made you want to cry just to think about it. You could climb one of the Tetons and stare almost to the Pacific and you wouldn't see nothing but maybe an Indian lodge or a small herd of buffalo. A man got so that he didn't want anything else. He just wanted to camp and ride and trap and maybe had himself a drink now and again and then rode off to be alone afterwards.' The old man sucked in a deep breath.

'I regret ever coming back. I should have left my hair up there and maybe the wolves would have eaten my bones. A man ain't no good, when he can't do the things he wants to do. Many's the time I've sat up at night and longed for my old rifle and a pinch of powder and a couple of charges. I'd like to stalk a buffalo like I did in the old days, creep up on him gentle and against the wind, draw a bead and send a ball just above his brisket. There's something satisfying in a man shooting a buffalo.'

He licked his lips.

'Then you run up and cut its throat and let it bleed. You skin it, belly down and starting from the hump. You gut it and look up and see the wolves and coyotes, all around just waiting for you to finish so they can get in and have themselves a feed. The magpies too, and the crows, all circling and ready to drop on what you leave. You'd take the liver and the hump and maybe a cut of rib-meat. You'd pick the fat and tasty parts and let the scavengers have the rest. Tender meat that was too, melt in the mouth raw or cooked, and it was meat that gave strength to a man and made him fit and strong.' The old man smacked his lips. 'Hell! The very thought of it makes me hungry.'

'When's chow?' Jud wasn't hungry but the old man's talk had disturbed him.

'About an hour. Hog meat, corn bread, beans and gravy.' The old man shrugged. 'Guess I'd better get on with it. Brenhardt will be back soon and him and his boys will be hungry.'

'How many men has he taken with him?'

'Couple of dozen.'

'How many here now?'

'With the guards and counting everyone I'd say no more than a score.'

'I see.' Jud nodded and watched the old man pick up his bucket and cross to the cook shack. He felt depressed, uneasy, irritated and on edge. The old man's talk had upset him with its picture of a time, just over thirty years ago, when the country was new and clean and waiting to be developed. Jud stared at his cigar, feeling the chill of the evening air close in around him, and thoughts chased around inside of his head as they had so often before.

The country had expanded too fast and that was the trouble. Thirty years had seen the trails open to the north, the Indians beaten and converted from fierce warriors to abject slaves. Some still retained their pride and many still rode the plains, scalping and burning in their eternal war with the white man, but the eastern Indians and those of the north had been vanquished and broken.

Steam boats had run up the Mississippi. Settlers had followed them and ground which had never known the touch of a plough was now under cultivation. Connestoga wagons had rolled west over the mountain passes of the north to Oregon and California, and others, taking the southern route, had met the incredible ferocity of the Apaches, Cheyennes, Sioux and Dakotas. They had fought those Indians, were still fighting, and while they fought the North and the South, instead of working together to build a new, fine nation, were locked in civil war.

It was a war of ideals and stubbornness. A Southerner himself, Jud knew that neither cause had right wholly on its side. While the South kept slaves and the North was free there would always be trouble. The nation was too big, too new for slavery to be tolerated once men had pushed back the frontiers. Slavery belonged to the old world, not the new, and so war had flared into a bitter struggle with each side striving to impose its will on the other.

And it had lasted for almost four years.

Four years in which the Confederated States had battled the Northern Union for the right to rule itself in its own way, a right the North refused to grant. For to allow that would be to split the country in two nations and, as Abraham Lincoln had said, that was a thing to be avoided at all costs. America had to grow as one unified whole, anything less would expose the new nation to the jealousies and invasions of hostile and greedy powers. For America was rich in land and gold and furs, things which all wanted and hoped to obtain. Let America be split into two countries and they would lose their precarious strength.

But one side had to lose, and soon, before the struggle ruined the entire eastern seaboard.

Jud, a Southerner, hoped that it would be the Confederated States which would prove victorious, but, as a man, he had his doubts.

As a soldier he had no doubts at all, only his duty. It was when he began thinking that his irritation increased. The utter stupidity of war, civil war at a time when the Indians to the West presented a common enemy, made him at times feel sick with the futility of destruction.

He dragged at his cigar, sending streamers of smoke into the still air. From the corral the sounds of horses as they drank echoed with startling clarity from the surrounding rocks. The smith, rested, took up his hammer and began pounding at horseshoes and the old man, ghostly in the twilight moved from store to cook shack, the light of his cooking fire casting a ruby glow on his leathery skin.

Jud dropped his cigar, crushed it beneath his heel, then turned as metal rang against rock. From the pass a file of horsemen came into the clearing. The man at their head, a squat, bearded, heavy-set character turned in his saddle and the sound of his voice filled the clearing.

'Step lively now, boys, we're home. I told you that I'd bring you back, didn't I? Trust old Brenhardt, he'll always see you safe.'

The men didn't answer. They rode

slumped in their saddles, almost all of them bearing the white splotch of crude bandages. They rode up to the corral, dismounted, unsaddled, sent their horses in with the others. Tiredly they carried their gear into the cabins and, after a while, a few of them came outside to the wash-house. Brenhardt himself, smelling of horse sweat and perspiration, gunsmoke and whiskey, came up to Jud and clapped him on the shoulder.

'Hi, Jud. Glad to see you.'

'Thanks.' Jud stared at the squat man, his eyes shadowed. 'Trouble?'

'Some, not more than we expected.'

'How many men did you take out?'

'Couple of dozen. Why?'

'You didn't bring that many back,' pointed out Jud. 'I counted them, you're six short.'

'So we ran into trouble,' said Brenhardt impatiently. 'A posse jumped us and we had to run for it. Some men got hurt and some got themselves killed. Am I to blame?'

'Maybe not, but Quantrill won't like it.'

'Then he can lump it. This is war, Jud, and in war men get hurt.' Brenhardt spat and wiped his beard on the back of his hand. 'How'd you make out?'

'So-so, and you?'

'Fair. I'll tell you about it later.' Brenhardt spat again. 'That dust! It clogs a man's throat until he'd give his soul for a good drink.'

'There's water in the creek.'

'When I talk of a drink I don't mean the stuff you fancy men wash in, I mean whiskey.' Brenhardt grinned as if joking but his eyes remained hard. 'Seen the boss yet?'

'Not yet.'

'Come in with me, we may as well tell one tale instead of repeating ourselves.' Brenhardt rubbed at his chin. 'Maybe I'll get me a swig of rotgut first, that ride clogged my throat and filled my ears. See you, Jud.'

'Brenhardt!'

'You said?'

'The drink can wait.' Jud stared at the man, making no attempt to hide his dislike. 'The first thing to do when returning from a ride is to report in. You know that. You know too that Quantrill doesn't like his officers filling themselves with rotgut when on duty.'

'So?'

'So you'd better report in with me.' Jud turned and led the way towards a small cabin against the rock. He knocked, pushed open the door, entered. A man looked up from where he was sitting.

Quantrill.

5

He was a small man. Slight, almost womanish in his delicate limbs and sensitive features, but a hint of the man's character was apparent in the liquid dark of his smouldering eyes. Strange eyes they were, seeming as if to contain a thousand trapped devils and the eyes, together with the short, clipped beard he favoured, gave him an air of the old world. Sitting behind his rough hewn desk he looked like one of the Spanish Grandees who had sailed the seas to settle the rich lands of Mexico, watching with hooded eyes as slaves were whipped to the bone for the good of their souls. A man who lived with an ideal, who fed it until it consumed him. Who fought and who would continue to fight until he finally yielded in the eternal sleep of death.

Quantrill! Hailed by the war-torn South as a brave patriot, cursed by the North as a brigand, an outlaw, feared by both North and South for the swift violence with which he struck, the unpredictable savagery of his attacks, the cold ruthlessness which had given rise to whispers of atrocities more hateful than any of those perpetrated by the Indians themselves.

He smiled as he saw Jud and his right hand lifted above the edge of his desk, the pistol it carried full-cocked and ready to kill. He uncocked it, slipped it back into its holster, and rising, gestured towards a chair.

'Captain Hawkins.' His odd eyes flickered. 'And Captain Brenhardt. Be seated gentlemen.'

Jud and the squat man took chairs and relaxed. Quantrill limped across to a cupboard, opened it, took out glasses and a bottle, a box of cigars and another of tobacco. He placed the things on the desk, poured drinks, offered cigars, stuffed a pipe, lit it, and held up his glass.

'Gentlemen! The South!'

They rose, drank the toast, and sat down again, Quantrill refilled the glasses.

'I am pleased to see you back, gentlemen, more pleased than I can say. I have had news, disturbing news, it may affect us deeply.' He spoke with a peculiar rounded resonance as of an educated man. His speech was tinged with the courtesy of the Old World, a heritage of his Spanish ancestry. His eyes, liquid and burning, were alive with inner thoughts. He drank, smoked, looked at Jud. 'Your report?'

'I ran into trouble.' said Jud. 'Bad trouble. The man I was escorting, Sam Calloway, got himself bitten by a rattler and died. I took his place and headed into Springfield. I took a chance, I don't look anything like Sam did, but I hoped that Thorne would contact me just the same.'

'A good man, Thorne,' said Quantrill. 'A pity about Sam. What happened?'

'Tending Sam had taken too much time and I reached Springfield almost too late for the rendezvous. I checked in the hotel, ordered a bath, and was contacted by a man calling himself Thorne. I'd never seen Thorne so wasn't certain if he was the right man or not. He knew the password but that meant nothing. He could have been a ringer as much as I was.' Jud sipped at his whiskey. 'He didn't know me but he didn't know that I wasn't Sam Calloway. He gave me instructions as to wrecking a train and tried to pump me. He was an agent of the Union.'

'So?'

'So I feared for my neck. The thing which gave me the tip was that he didn't seem interested in money.' Jud reached under his shirt and tossed a heap of greenbacks on the desk. 'He didn't ask for his pay. I dodged out and made as if I was going to contact you. Naturally they tried to tail me. I gave them the slip, doubled back, and planted a couple of bombs. I managed to blow up the railhead and destroy a warehouse full of ammunition. That's on the credit side. On the other is the fact that we've lost our paid spy in Springfield, the Union is suspicious, and we can expect trouble the next time we try anything similar.'

'I see.' Quantrill looked at the pile of bills. 'You did well, Captain. You managed to carry out our plan even though they were suspicious of you. I shall mention you in dispatches.' He reached out and touched the pile of money.

'I had to use some,' said Jud. 'I wasn't too sure how close they were after me so I took a long circle and rode easy. That's why I'm so late. I could have been here a week ago but I figured that it wasn't worth it. I took the opportunity to do a little scouting and looking around on the way. We aren't as popular as we used to be.'

'I know it.' Quantrill took up the money, rose, and tossed it into a chest. 'These fools forget that we are fighting their war. Even if we are independents and dispense with uniforms. They refuse to see that by helping us they are helping the entire Confederacy. It's getting to the point where we have to pay for everything we need, horses, blankets, medical supplies, everything. Even information and assistance.' He sat down again, wincing as he bumped his leg. 'Brenhardt?'

'According to plan. We entered the town and strung out like I suggested. We jumped the bank just as the stage rolled in from the gold fields. We had a little trouble but managed to shoot our way clear. We got the dust and a heap of greenbacks, some Confederate money too.'

'Losses?'

'Six men.'

'That's bad.' Quantrill drummed his fingers on the desk. 'Where is the money now?'

'In my saddle-bags, I'll bring it in later.' The squat man reached for the bottle and poured himself a drink without waiting for an invitation. 'A posse came after us and we had to fight our way clear. I'd guess that we took about a dozen men for our six.' He drank, reached for the bottle, drank again. Quantrill watched him, frowning and biting his lip.

'Six men gone,' said Jud thoughtfully. 'We've got thirty-eight men left, Quantrill. Not many to fight a war.'

'We'll get by,' said Brenhardt. He spoke thickly as if the whiskey were taking quick effect.

'We started with over two hundred,' said Jud as if the other man hadn't spoken. 'Volunteers from Texas and Louisiana. We had officers from the regular army, men like Jelkson, and Yendle. They died and we didn't get others to replace them.'

'We couldn't,' said Quantrill. 'The South needed every trained man they could get.'

'We don't need them,' snorted Brenhardt. 'We can do without your fancy officers and their ideas. This is rough country and we have to use rough men. We need men born to the desert and hills, who can ride all day every day, who can shoot from the hip and hit what they aim at. Men like me.'

'You're not an army man,' said Jud. 'You don't count.'

'I'm a Captain, ain't I?'

'Only because we made you one.'

'So what?' Brenhardt set down his glass, his eyes ugly. 'You trying to crow over me, Jud? Just because you once wore a fancy grey outfit with a sword and a row of medals. Does that make you a better man than me?'

'It makes me a soldier,' said Jud. 'I can fight the enemy because they are the enemy. I can blow up trains and kill fresh-faced kids and stain the dirt with their blood and that's all right because I'm a soldier and that's what soldiers do in time of war. I don't need a uniform to do that. What are you, Brenhardt? You drifted in here with a couple of men and said that you wanted to volunteer. We took you and made you a captain because this is supposed to be a part of the Confederate army. And what do you do? You ride out and rob a bank.'

'I ordered that,' said Quantrill quickly. 'We need money, Jud, cash money, greenbacks to bribe our northern spies and to buy supplies. How else could we get it?'

'I don't know,' admitted Jud. 'Maybe I'm wrong but to me all this is dirty and bad. I do it because that's what I'm here for but I don't have to like it.'

'You're tired,' said Quantrill. 'I know how you feel. I should have ridden with you myself and would have done if it hadn't been for this leg.' He stared at it. 'Still, it's healed now and I can sit a horse. The next time we raid I'll be leading you.'

Jud nodded, sipping his drink, his eyes dark with thought. Brenhardt snorted and emptied his glass.

'Talk like that makes me sick in the belly,' he said. 'Hell, this is war, ain't it? What does it matter what we do or how we do it so long as it hurts the enemy? We need money, all right so we take it. Does that make us wrong? Every dollar we take from the North helps the South by just that much. Seems to me, Jud, that you've turned soft all of a sudden. You didn't used to be like this back in the old days.'

'You're talking of a year ago,' said Jud. 'That's when you rode in and asked to join. I've had a lot more of it than that. I've been fighting four years now and I'm getting tired of it.'

'We are all getting tired of it,' said Quantrill. 'But we'll go on fighting until we either win or they bury us. We stand for the South and while I'm alive the South will never be beaten. No, by God! Not if I have to fight alone with my bare hands! I'll fight the North until they beat me to death because that's the only way they will stop me.' He paused, twin spots of red glowing in his shallow cheeks, and his eyes seemed to leap and surge with hidden fires.

'Thirty-eight men,' said Jud. 'Not many.'

'We'll get more,' said Brenhardt. 'There's many a cowpuncher would like to ride with us and that's not all. We can get the owlhoots, the wild men, the . . . '

'No!'

'Why not, Jud? What difference does it make?'

'This difference,' said Jud tightly. 'I used to be proud of riding with Quantrill. I thought it was something good and smart and useful to the Cause. I didn't aim to ride with no range-scum and outlaws. I've heard talk about us which would shrivel your ears if you heard it. Talk from our own people as well as the Northerners. You know what they think of us? They think of us as if we were a bunch of coyotes.' He shrugged. 'Sure, the Southerners to the east don't think of us like that. They think we're doing something wonderful, but they don't have to supply us with horses, food, ammunition and money.

They can sit back and give orders and act the gentleman. I tell you, Quantrill, there's only one thing which will justify what we've done, and that is to win the war. Lose it, and our necks will be a fair mark for a noose.'

'That is a risk we have always taken,' said Quantrill, calmly. He puffed at his pipe, prodded a finger in the bowl, scowled and putting it by lit a cigar. 'You're upset, Jud, and I understand how you feel. We are different from the others, you and I. We are officers of the Confederate army, trained men, uniformed and commissioned. We have chosen to conduct a guerrilla war. I think that we chose wisely, I have always said that a small, picked body of mounted men could harry the enemy better than a full regiment of regular troops.'

'A lot of good your uniforms and commissions will do you if you're ever caught,' said Brenhardt. 'They'll dangle you just as high.'

'I know it.' Quantrill shook his head

as if dismissing an unpleasant subject. 'Enough of this talk. I told you that I had news. Unfortunately it is bad news. Sherman smashed our lines at Gettysburg and is marching through Georgia.'

He stared at the two men, his liquid eyes burning in the reflected light of the lamp. In the sudden silence the sounds of the camp sounded magnified and all out of proportion. Jud could hear the stamping of the horses, the little sounds the smith made as he put away his tools, the clatter from the cook shack and even the groans of wounded men as they eased their hurts. He swallowed and, when he spoke, his voice sounded strange to his ears.

'When?'

'A runner from the telegraph office brought me the news at dawn. He had ridden all night. By now Sherman must be tearing the South with his armies on his way to the sea. General Lee is our only hope now, that and what we can do to aid the South.'

'What?'

'I have a plan.' Quantrill reached behind him and unrolled a map. 'I've thought of what to do should this happen for a long time now, ever since the tide of war began to turn against us. We are too small to inflict much damage, too remote to change the course of war, but there are ways in which we can help to repair the damage.' He paused and, in the lamplight, his face suddenly became thin and cruel.

'We can hit these damn Yankees where it hurts them the most. In their pockets.'

Jud sucked in a deep breath, only now beginning to realize the full extent of the news. In his mind's eye he had a sudden picture of a swarm of blue-coated soldiers flooding over the South. They would be ruthless, those soldiers, they had suffered too many defeats, the war had bitten too deeply for them to have remembered mercy or the fact that they were fighting their own. The slaves, too, the negroes held in bondage by the Southern owners, they would rise at the taste of freedom and . . .

He became aware of what Quantrill was saying.

'I have made careful plans and I think that with care, we will have a good chance of success. My spies tell me that the payroll will be taken to St Louis and from there conducted under strong guard down to Memphis. From what I can learn there is close to a million dollars in greenbacks in that consignment, money to pay the troops and to keep the war going.' Quantrill rolled up the map. 'If we can capture that money then we will have struck a great blow for freedom. With it we can slip across the border and hire Mexican mercenaries to fight for us. We can buy guns and medical supplies for the shattered army. With that million dollars we can equip a strong force of guerrillas to harry the enemy as far North as Ohio. We can keep the war going and, maybe, we can provide just that little extra the South needs to turn the balance.'

'A million dollars!' Brenhardt reached for the bottle and his glass rang against his teeth as he drank. 'In greenbacks, you said?'

'That's right. Nice new bills direct from the Government mint.'

'A million dollars!' Brenhardt couldn't seem to get over it. 'And you reckon we can reach out and grab it?'

'Yes.'

'Man, that's real money!' The squat man grinned and licked his lips. 'With money like that who cares for anything?'

'It's for the Cause,' said Quantrill sharply. 'Every dollar of it goes into the war-chest.'

'Sure.' Brenhardt winked and rubbed his fingers against his thumb. 'Naturally.' He chuckled. 'I get it. I get it good.'

Quantrill stared at Brenhardt for a long moment, then looked at Jud.

'It will need careful planning,' he

said. 'And we will have to move fast. I have worked on taking thirty men with us, two horses for each man. We will ride Indian style and should be able to cover ground at the rate of a hundred to a hundred and fifty miles a day. We will strike fast, ride swiftly, and be safe before they know what has happened. Once we have the money I will send word to the South and they can contact agents across the border.'

'We can't take thirty men,' said Jud. 'Brenhardt lost six and most of his party were wounded. I'd say that we can maybe manage a score at the most. Some will have to stay behind to guard the camp.'

'They will have to do.' Quantrill nodded as if, in his mind, he had already altered his arrangements to take care of the reduced number. He sighed. 'Men are our problem. We need fresh recruits and we need them fast.'

'I can take care of them,' said Brenhardt. 'Give me a few dollars and a couple of men and I'll round you up as tough a bunch as you could wish for. They may not be willing to ride with you and play at soldiers, but let me tell them that we're after the folding money and you'll have an army waiting to sign up.' He grinned. 'Experienced men too, most of them.'

'Outlaws,' said Jud and shook his head. 'No.'

'Why not?'

'There are reasons why not, reasons you maybe wouldn't understand.' He looked at Quantrill. 'When do we ride?'

'Tomorrow at sunset. We'll ride all night and as far as we can. Time's short and I want to get moving again.' Quantrill scowled down at his leg. 'I've been laid up too long.'

'You were lucky not to have been laid up for good,' said Brenhardt. 'That slug could have taken off your leg or aimed a mite higher, smashed your hip.' He shook his head. 'A man don't ride none with a shattered hip.'

Quantrill shrugged, not answering, his eyes heavy with brooding thought.

He stared over at Brenhardt, then at Jud, and seemed about to say something when the ringing clatter of the cook's tripod echoed over the clearing.

'Chow.' The squat man heaved himself to his feet. 'I'm hungry.' He nodded to Quantrill and dived for the door and Jud could hear his heavy voice yelling to the cook as he made his way to the cook shack.

'How bad is it?'

'How bad is what?'

'You know what I mean,' said Jud. He stared at the dark-eyed man at his side. 'The news. I've been out of circulation for a couple of weeks and I know how fast an army can travel once it smashes the resistance. How bad are we?'

'Bad,' said Quantrill. 'Very bad. We couldn't hold the Yankees and they crushed us at Gettysburg. That much I know for certain. How far Sherman has advanced into Georgia is anyone's guess but one thing is certain, he won't show mercy. You know Sherman as well as I do, a hard, ruthless man. To him opposition is something to be crushed, wiped out without hesitation, and he will use his army to ruin the South. I know that army, Jud. They aren't the gentlemen soldiers we used to fight at the outbreak of war. Most of them are prison-sweepings, toughs, any and everyone who can hold a gun and kill an enemy. They've been impressed to replace those we killed and they are raring to go. They will sweep through the South like a flame and Sherman will encourage them to loot and burn and kill. He will do that because he daren't give us time to recover. He will get us on the run and keep us on the run and he will make sure that, even if we beat him back, the South will be devastated so as to bring us to our knees sooner or later.'

'I see.' Jud stared out of the open door to where the men sat hunched around the fires eating their beans, hog meat, corn bread and gravy. 'In other words, Quantrill, the South has lost the war, is that it?'

'No, Jud. We haven't lost. We will never lose while a single man is willing to fight and die for the Cause. Things are bad but we can recover.' The dark-eyed man smiled and slapped Jud on the shoulder. 'Go and eat now, have a drink or two and get some sleep. I want you fresh for tomorrow so that we can discuss the plans.' He smiled again. 'And don't worry.'

'No,' said Jud. 'I won't do that.'

He stepped from the cabin and made his way towards the cooking fires.

6

The camp was silent except for the occasional mutter of one man to another and the clink of spoons against metal plates. They were eating cold, spooning up soggy beans and greasy bacon, swallowing it down with water laced with whiskey, and chewing on husks of corn bread dipped in cold beanjuice. Some of the men, their meal finished, lay on their backs and stared upwards, some of them sucking on empty pipes, a few chewing dead cigars, others busy with their chaws of tobacco. A few steps away the horses, nuzzling the ground for what grass they could find, stamped and moved restlessly in the chill bite of the night wind.

Quantrill wiped his plate with a piece of bread, ate it, poured himself a slug of whiskey, added a little water and gulped it down. Sucking his empty pipe he rose and walked to where Jud stood, a dim shadow among shadows, his eyes alert as he faced the east.

The moon had long set and the stars, glittering like a double handful of diamonds tossed by some careless jeweller on the black velvet of the sky, cast a thin and ghostly illumination over the rolling plain, the scrub, the stunted trees and the distant hills. The camp was in a gully, sheltered even during the day from direct sight and, as Quantrill turned, he could see nothing but the dark hump of a patch of bush, smell nothing but the sage and the scent of horses, hear nothing but the low mutter as one man spoke to another.

Aside from himself and the man at his side the world seemed empty and devoid of life.

'Quiet,' said Jud softly. 'Not a coyote or a dog. Not a man or horse in all the world. Gets you, don't it?'

Quantrill nodded, not wanting to speak, just wanting to stand and breathe and feel the terrifying immensity of the empty night enter his soul. It was at times like this that he felt really himself. It was now that a man could really feel alive, alone and free with the world waiting for him to leave his mark. It was a good thing he was doing, he knew it and knowing it regretted nothing. He didn't miss his uniform, the life he could have had in camp and barrack, the endless confusion of regular war, the superior officers, the underlings, the fools who ruined careful plans through ignorance and fear. He had left all that behind him and now, as he stood on the edge of the plain, he was his own master, free to go his own way. He felt even taller as he thought about it.

'Dawn isn't far off,' murmured Jud. 'We'd better get into position at the first light.'

'Time enough for that,' said Quantrill. He came barely to the big man's shoulder but his voice was calm with self-confidence. 'Let the men get what rest they can. Once we start moving there'll be no rest until we're back at

Ranthorne.' He stared up at Jud. 'You eaten?'

'Yes.'

'Maybe you'd better get some rest?'

'I'll manage.' Jud felt in his pocket and pulled out a cigar. He rolled it, smelt it, stuck it between his lips. 'You'll have to count me out during the first light, Quantrill,' he said. 'I want to check the dynamite.'

'Will we need it?'

'Maybe not, but I want to make sure just the same.'

'You and your giant powder,' chuckled Quantrill. 'When I asked for a man with knowledge of explosives I didn't reckon on getting an engineer. What were you before the war, Jud? Prospector?'

'You said it the first time,' said Jud. 'I was an engineer, a good one though I say so myself. I learned to handle dynamite as other men learned to handle horses or pan gold.'

'Is that why you carry a couple of sticks about with you?' Quantrill shook his head. 'Ain't you afraid that it will go off and blow you to Kingdom Come before your time?'

'Dynamite is safe enough if you know how to use it,' said Jud. 'I carry high-shock stuff, it takes a detonator to blow it off. Why, I've seen old-timers use it to light fires, even hammer it and once I saw a man fire a bullet into a stick. Nothing happened. Most people don't know it but it takes more than just a knock to set it off. You have to have a detonator to do the job properly.'

'I'm not arguing,' said Quantrill. 'You can take time to get your bombs ready, all the time you need, but I doubt if we'll need them.'

Jud shrugged and both men fell silent as they stared towards the east. Above their heads the stars began to fade, the Big Dipper swinging about the Pole Star as the night passed on and, gradually, the dark of the night yielded to an oyster grey.

The light brightened, gaining strength from the east, and when the ground and plain was clear, Quantrill moved.

Going back to the camp he aroused the men who, shivering a little, rose and beat their hands together to restore warmth and feeling. The horses were watered, fed a handful of corn, and readied for immediate travel. The men themselves checked their weapons, opening the side gates of their Colts and spinning the chambers to make sure that each held one of the big, round-nosed bullets. The rifles too were checked then, as the light grew stronger, Quantrill gave his orders.

'Brenhardt. Take six men and ride up to that patch of scrub. Take cover and don't move until you hear me yell.'

'Why's that?' asked the squat man. His breath was sour with too much whiskey. Quantrill looked impatient.

'The money will be in convoy and well guarded,' he explained. 'They will have a vanguard, then the wagon and escort, then a rearguard. If they have any sense they may have a second rearguard coming well after the first. I want you to hold back as a reserve. I want you to let the van and escort pass, watch for the rear, check to make sure that there are no other soldiers in sight, then cut loose with your rifles. Hold your shots until we start the firing, and don't ride out until I give the word. Understand?'

'Sure.'

'I hope so.' Quantrill looked at Jud. 'You take six men and be ready to attack the escort. I'll take the rest and ride down the trail apiece. Don't wait for me. You start shooting as soon as the escort come up to you. Shoot fast, get the money, and don't worry about the rest. I'll take care of the vanguard and Brenhardt will take care of the rear.'

Jud nodded but Brenhardt didn't seem too happy.

'Seems crazy to me,' he said. 'Why split our forces at all? Why not ride down on them in a bunch, shoot them to pieces, grab the cash and run? Seems to me that by splitting us up you'll get into trouble. Those soldier boys can shoot and they will outnumber us for sure.'

'That's what you would think,' snapped Quantrill. 'That's why outlaws don't last long and why the Indians lose every war they fight with the military. Bunch us up and we'll be a nice, big, sitting target. My way, the proper way, we shoot from cover, have the element of surprise, and weaken all their forces at the same time. What's the good of wiping out the escort if we don't touch the front and rear guards? They'll ride in on us and we'll be between two fires.' He stared over the plain. 'Better get moving. Remember, use rifles and fire in volley not as individuals. Reload and keep firing as long as you can. Don't break cover unless you have to and don't start banging off your six-guns without doing some damage. Take it slow and easy, pick your target, wait for the word, then cut 'em down. Right. To your positions!'

Brenhardt nodded, mounted his

horse and, calling to his men, rode to the north and a patch of scrub. Quantrill watched him go then, smiling at Jud, took another six men and rode south. They had already scouted the ground and Jud knew that Quantrill's men would find cover a little south. He, himself, made sure that his men and their horses were out of sight and then, climbing to the ridge of the gully, settled down to wait.

While waiting he checked his dynamite. He cut two sticks into small portions, attached short lengths of fuse, and primed the charges ready for detonation. He slipped a fresh cigar between his teeth, lit it, and made sure that no smoke rose from the end. Satisfied that it was well alight and burning steadily, he set it down and, narrowing his eyes, stared into the distance.

It was a long wait.

The sun climbed above the horizon and swung above the plain and, as it rose, so the chill of the night was replaced by the growing heat of the day. Higher climbed the sun, still higher, until it hung at high noon. Jud crouched waiting with the patience of an Indian, replacing his cigar with fresh ones when the old one burned out and, as the day dragged and still no sign of the soldiers was to be seen, some of the men began to grumble at the long inactivity.

'You think they're coming, Jud?' One of the men, a bow-legged Texan, climbed up beside the watching man. 'Sure think myself that Quantrill bought a bum steer. This waiting's getting me down.'

'They'll be here,' said Jud.

'It's possible that they won't,' argued the man. 'How long do we wait, Jud?'

'All day if necessary. All night and all the next day too.'

'That's a mighty long wait.'

'Talking won't make it shorter.' Jud stiffened, his eyes on the distance. 'See anything?'

'Haze,' grunted the Texan. He frowned.

'It ain't so either. Reminds me of a herd of cows moving or . . . '

'A body of horses,' Jud nodded. 'It's them. Get the men up on the ridge, make sure that their rifles don't catch the sun and keep their heads down until I give the word. Move!'

The Texan nodded and, dropping back, gave quick instructions to the waiting men. Jud, tense on watch, stared at the distant cloud of dust, hitched his rifle to a more convenient position, then slumped down until only his eyes were visible.

The dust grew nearer.

Sounds grew with it, the thud of hooves and the jingle of spurs, the little sounds made by sabres touching the stirrup irons and the unmistakable creak and rumble of a fast wagon.

Jud ducked lower as the vanguard passed, ten mounted soldiers, armed and riding with long stirrups and loose reins. They talked as they rode, joking and sitting as if they didn't have an enemy in the world. A young sergeant rode with them, his boyish face keen and eager as he led the way. They passed, riding by in a plume of dust, and Jud raised himself, signalling to his men, tensing as he gripped his rifle.

The wagon and the main escort came nearer. The wagon was a strong, flat-bedded affair, big-wheeled and harnessed to a couple of deep-chested bays. A box rode behind the driver's seat, a square, locked, formidable box hooped and banded with straps of metal. With the driver rode a non-com, his rifle in his hands. To either side of the wagon was the escort, ten men a side and, before the wagon, a young lieutenant sat his horse as though he were leading the army of Alexander to the conquest of the known world.

Jud reached down and picked up his cigar. He puffed it, took a bomb from his pocket, laid it ready to hand. He whispered swift instructions.

'Get ready to fire. Aim at the escort counting from left to right. Aim good and loose easy. I want to see five of them down at the first volley and five at the second.'

'What about the wagon?' The Texan sucked in his breath as he squinted through the dust. 'Those horses will bolt at the first shot.'

'I'll attend to that. Ready now, fire on the word.'

Jud had been watching the progress of the wagon, his eyes hard with calculation. He picked up the bomb, waited until his eyes measured time and distance, then, touching the fuse to the cigar between his teeth, he threw the little package of dynamite down the trail. Immediately he picked up his rifle, aimed, and tightened his finger on the trigger.

'Fire!'

The shots roared as one, the smoke from the burning powder rolling to mingle with the dust. Men screamed as hot lead blasted into them, the horses whinnied, reared, and the yelling of the officer came thinly through the dust.

'Down!' Jud turned and yelled the

warning. 'Down!' He flung himself beneath the edge of the gully.

Above him the sweating wagon driver fought his horses, fought and failed as, with the bit between their teeth, they lunged away from the smoke and noise. Three yards they ran, three short yards, then horses and wagon lifted on a column of smoke and flame and thunder as the bomb roared beneath them. Immediately Jud leapt for the edge of the gully, his men with him, and their rifles lifted and fired as one.

Desperately they reloaded, flinging back the breechblock and thumbing fresh cartridges into the chambers of their carbines. Training would have made the manoeuvre second nature, the hard, rigorous training of the military, but as it was only Jud and the Texan reloaded in time. Their rifles flamed as the escort, recovering a little from the sound and fury of sudden death, twisted, spurred, and rode towards the hidden men.

Two of them died in the saddle.

Three others ducked as hastily-aimed lead whined over their shoulders, then they had reached the gully, had jumped it, and the air filled to the snarling roar of six-guns.

It was almost slaughter. It was gun against gun, the dismounted man against mounted, and the dismounted lying in cover, able to take better aim and fire with more ease, shot the soldiers from their saddles as if they had been clay pigeons at a fair. The soldiers fought back, jerking at their reins as their horses, wounded and frightened, stamped and reared and tried to bolt. The stamping and rearing made it impossible for them to aim the long pistols in their hands, made it worse than useless for them to draw their sabres. Men and horses died to the rolling thunder of controlled death, to the surge of powder smoke and the snarl of hot lead.

But they did not die alone.

Next to Jud the Texan gasped, swore, tried to rise then fell back with an ugly hole in his chest. A second man, his gun raised to fire, toppled with a foolish expression on his face and a hole between his eyes. Two others screamed as lead tore into them, screamed, and fired at the soldiers until their guns were empty.

Suddenly it was all over.

A few horses rolled at the bottom of the gully, their screaming making the day hideous with noise. Blue uniformed shapes sprawled on the dusty ground, some dead, others wounded, while from the gully the unmounted horses ran with furious whinnying and rolling eyes. Jud glanced around, his fingers thrusting fresh cartridges into the chambers of his pistol. He looked over the edge of the gully, the wagon lay toppled to one side, two blue-uniformed figures lying next to the dead horses which had pulled it. From the south came the sound of shots and the thunder of hooves while, from the north where Brenhardt had waited, the spiteful crack of rifle fire echoed from the plain.

Turning, Jud dropped into the gully and, with three quick shots, stilled the screaming of the dying horses as hot lead put them out of their misery. Of his own men only two were able to stand, one of them wounded in the arm. Together they raced for their horses, mounted and, with guns fresh-loaded and at the ready, spurred towards the south.

Quantrill was in trouble.

He had had poor cover and had been seen. Half of his men had been shot from the saddle at the first encounter and, when Jud arrived, the little man was fighting for his life. Jud and the two men with him charged up to the mêlée, fired, fired again and, suddenly, the area was free of uniforms aside from those sprawled on the ground.

'Good work.' Quantrill glanced about him, his eyes counting the men. 'Seven dead! We must join with Brenhardt.'

Jud noded and led the way towards the mounting sounds of rifle fire.

It stilled as they swung past the

destroyed wagon and Brenhardt, his face streaming with blood from a scalp wound, came galloping to join them. Behind him rode his men, two wounded and swaying in the saddle. Quantrill checked his mount and counted the men.

'Two dead.'

'They stuck their necks out,' said Brenhardt, and spat. 'Fools, all they had to do was to crouch down and keep firing.' He grinned. 'Our first volley caught them in the rear. Then the dynamite went off and startled them, we cut down a couple more before they knew what hit them. The rest was easy.'

'Survivors?'

'None.'

Quantrill nodded and led the way back to the toppled wagon. 'Get those spare horses up here. See if you can do anything for the wounded. See if there are any survivors.' He looked at Jud. 'Get that box open.'

The explosion had loosened the joints of the box but, bad as the detonation had been, the metal straps had held. Jud examined it, stared at the stout lock, then drew his pistol from its holster. Five shots he slammed against the hasp, using the bullets as he would a giant hammer, and on the fifth shot the metal yielded and gave way. Quickly he jerked the box open, stared inside, then nodded to Quantrill.

'Here it is.'

'The money!' Brenhardt shoved forward, his eyes eager. He whistled as he stared at the neatly packaged heap of newly-printed bills. 'So that's what a million dollars looks like!'

'Get it in the saddlebags,' snapped Jud curtly. He stared over the plain, his eyes thoughtful as his fingers, as if with life of their own, automatically refilled the chambers of his pistol. Quantrill nodded to the squat man and watched for a while as men, sweating in their eagerness, stuffed the money into the saddlebags they had brought with them.

'What do you think, Jud?'

'Messy.' Jud stared around him at the litter of broken bodies and dead horses. 'Too much like the front line. This trail must be well-travelled by the look of it for all that we haven't seen anyone else. My guess is that we were lucky; that luck may not last, let's get moving.'

'Sure.' Quantrill stared over the plain. 'I'll just check to see if there are any survivors and then we'll hit the trail.'

'Say, Quantrill!' A man stopped and held something up in the air. 'Take a look at this rifle. Sure seems different to the ones we use.'

'It's a Winchester.' Quantrill took the weapon and examined it. 'Collect all you can. Are any of these Yankees alive?'

'Sure. There's a couple down in the gully still breathing and some more up here. One of them's the officer.'

'Kill them.'

'Wait!' Jud stepped forward. 'None of that, Quantrill. This may be war but we fight it according to the rules. We can't take prisoners but there's no need for murder. If some are still alive we'll leave them that way.'

'And have them arouse the troops on us?'

'Why not?' Jud stared at the small man. 'Listen, Quantrill, and listen good. I've stuck with you up to now because you've fought the game square. We are at war, all right, then let's fight as men and not as Indians. We stood to kill or be killed, leave it at that.'

'If they had won they would have hung us to the nearest tree.' Quantrill's eyes burned with rage. 'Is that fair?'

'Maybe, maybe not, but the risk is of our own making.'

'You're a weak-bellied fool, Jud,' said Quantrill coldly. 'This is no game for weaklings. This is war, war to the death and I don't give any quarter.'

'You do as you please,' said Jud softly. His lips thinned and a muscle jumped high on one cheek. 'I'm not asking you, Quantrill, I'm telling you. Kill those wounded men and your horse goes back without a rider.'

'This is mutiny, Jud, you know that?'

'I'm a soldier,' said Jud slowly. 'I go by the rules. Killing wounded men isn't one of them.' His hand dropped to the gun at his waist. 'I ride with you, Quantrill, but I'm not your dog. Play the game square or we part here and now.'

For a moment the two men stared at each other, will against will, and Jud knew with a sickening certainty that the small man would never back down. He stiffened his own resolve then, just as the tension had almost reached the breaking point, one of the wounded men, the officer, groaned and stirred and opened his eyes. He blinked, tried to sit up, then sank back, his lips white with pain from a shattered leg.

'You murdering scum,' he rasped. 'Attacking the United States Cavalry. You'll hang for this.'

'Maybe.'

'I suppose that you're going to kill me.' The officer stared up at Jud and Quantrill. 'That's all you can do now. If you don't then the entire army will be hunting for you.'

'You Yankees have been doing that for four years now,' sneered Quantrill. 'I'm still alive and able to fight.'

'We'll get you,' promised the officer. 'You can't do things like this and get away with it, you damn outlaw. There's law in this country and it'll make you pay.'

'Whose law!' Jud stared down at the officer. 'Don't worry about getting killed, we won't harm you. We aren't outlaws or drifters. We are a part of the Confederate Army. Maybe you've heard of us, Quantrill's raiders?'

'I've heard of you,' admitted the officer, his eyes looked puzzled.

'Then you know all about us,' said Jud. For some reason he felt it important to justify himself before this wounded man. Maybe it was pride, the strange affinity between officers no matter to which army they belonged, or perhaps it was because he wanted to wash the scorn from the helpless man's eyes. 'This was a battle,' he explained. 'You are our enemy, the enemy of the Confederacy, and we are Southern soldiers fighting for what we believe to be the right Cause. Maybe you feel the same about the North, I wouldn't know, but we aren't outlaws or murderers but soldiers. Can you understand that?'

'Let's get away from here,' said Quantrill.

'I want him to understand,' said Jud. He looked at the officer. 'We don't wear uniforms and we ride rough but we are as much a part of the Confederate Army as General Lee himself.'

'We're wasting time,' said Quantrill. 'The money is loaded and the men are waiting. Let's get moving, Jud, before someone spots us and collects a posse.'

'I'm coming.' Jud looked again at the officer. 'I'm sorry we had to ambush you, but you might have expected it. Things like that happen all the time in war. Remember it and, when you meet the enemy, take better care.'

'What enemy?'

'Us.' Jud frowned. 'The Confederate Army, the South, that's what you would call your enemy.'

'Not me.' The officer licked his lips, his face registering both bewilderment and contempt. 'A pretty speech, mister, but it won't wash. You and all your talk of war. Just talk to make yourselves look big. What war?'

'The Civil War,' snapped Jud. 'What else?'

'You doggone fool,' said the officer slowly. 'Don't you know? There ain't no war. It's finished, over, peace was signed between General Grant and General Lee a week ago. The South lost. The war's over.'

It was like hearing the end of the world.

7

Captain Sam Wayland, no longer dressed in the trim blue of the Northern Union, lounged at a bar in a saloon two days' ride from Texas, and tried not to worry about his lack of progress. Trailing Quantrill was not the easiest thing in the world. Even wearing the chaps and shirt of a roving cowhand, even with the low-slung six-gun of a drifter he still didn't feel the part he was supposed to be playing. Captain Leman, also in disguise, tasted his whiskey, pulled a face, then bravely drank it down.

Leman was inclined to regard the whole thing as fun. He had spent long hours practising the draw and he fancied himself as a gunman. Sam, more wise in the ways of the South, had tried to disillusion him.

Now, as he leaned on the long bar

and drank and let his eyes drift over the few men occupying the saloon, he felt a sense of failure. Everyone seemed to know of Quantrill but no one seemed to know where he was to be found. He rode like a ghost, struck, vanished, only to strike again. Even now that the war was over the Southerners were disinclined to give more information. Sam could understand that, it had happened too fast, was too sudden for the full realization of defeat to have sunk in. Not that it would affect the Texans so much, but further east the shock of defeat would have bitten deep. He wondered how it would affect Quantrill.

A man entered the saloon, a desert rat by his appearance, one of the prospectors who braved the deserts with a mule and a pack in their eternal search for gold. He stamped the dust from his faded boots, wiped the back of his hand over his bearded mouth, and stared about him with little, shrewd eyes. He was after a free drink or a greenhorn who would grub-stake him for another search of the desert. He looked at Sam.

'Hi, stranger,' he wheezed. 'You new to town?'

'Rode in a couple of hours ago.' Sam didn't look at Leman as he spoke. As far as anyone knew they were strangers and he wanted things to remain that way. 'Have a drink?'

'That's sure kind of ye,' said the old man. He watched as the bartender poured out a measure of whiskey. 'Here's mud in your eye.'

Sam nodded, poured another drink from the bottle the bartender, Western style, had left on the counter. 'Any luck?'

'Tanned a mite of dust from Old Hightop,' said the old man. His eyes gleamed. 'There's sure a heap of pay-dirt in them hills. If I had me a grub-stake I reckon I could strike the mother-lode and bring back nuggets as big as your fist.' He gulped at his drink. 'Sure be a smart man who'd risk maybe

131

a thousand dollars on a grub-stake.' He peered at Sam. 'Half what I find and no trouble at all, you know the way it is.'

Sam nodded. He knew what the old prospector was getting at. Under Western law anyone who supplied a prospector with a grub-stake, funds for him to buy food and supplies for a search in the desert or mountains, was legally entitled to half of what his partner found. Some men had grown rich that way, staking the old-timers and taking their share of dust and nuggets, but most regarded it as a pleasant form of charity, hardly worth the thousand to one chance of the prospector finding anything of real value. In any case no grub-stake would run to as high as a thousand dollars. Sam said so and the old man shrugged.

'I need a couple of mules, some bacon and giant powder, tools and other gear. Maybe I could buy cheap and do it for say five hundred. Interested?'

'Not at that price.'

'I could make it less,' urged the old man. 'For a couple of hundred I could pan out enough dust to pay you back double.'

'Forget it.' Sam turned to the bar and reached for the bottle. 'If you want some easy money better contact Quantrill. He picked up a cool million on that raid against the Army. Ask him for a hand-out, he's got more than I have!'

'Quantrill's a smart man,' said the old-timer. 'Yes, sir, a real smart man.' He chuckled. 'Made them Yankees pretty sick to lose all that money, I bet.'

'Quantrill is a wind-bag,' said Sam deliberately. 'So he was lucky, so what? Does that make him something special? He took that coin a week ago and what has he done with it? If you ask me he's salting away so that he can spend it in comfort later on. What makes me sick is to hear some people talking about him as though he were something special.'

Sam was risking an argument and he knew it but he was tired of looking for a

phantom and any action, even dangerous action, was better than this sheer,
frustrating waste of time.

He got his argument.

A man at the end of the bar, a silent,
whip-like man, raised his head and
stared at Sam.

'You talking about Quantrill?'

'Sure, what of it?'

'Seems to me that you're pretty
loose-mouthed in what you say.' The
man straightened from the bar and
moved towards Sam. 'Suppose I told
you that Quantrill is a friend of mine?'

'Some men pick strange friends,' said
Sam deliberately. 'I knew a man once
who swore by a coyote and another who
liked to pet a rattler. Trouble was the
rattler didn't seem to know just how
friendly that man was. Leastways he up
and bit him just the same.'

'Meaning?'

'Meaning thay maybe Quantrill isn't
so much a friend of yours as you seem
to think.'

'Lippy, ain't you.'

'No.' Sam stared at the man. 'Don't get me wrong. It just seems to me that Quantrill's a mighty hard man to locate, a greedy one at that. Me, I'd be willing to let a few men into the game and deal high. Especially if they was friends of mine — or said they were.'

'Talk don't mean nothing,' snapped the man. He stared at Sam as if registering him in his mind. 'I don't recollect ever seeing you before. Someone once told me that it was bad luck to shoot strangers so I'm not aiming to kill you without cause. Eat your words or reach for your iron!'

Sam took a deep breath and looked around the saloon. Men stood at the bar, their eyes watchful as they looked at him. Before him the whip-like man stood, his feet slightly parted, his arms loose at his side, his body crouched a little. It was the gunfighter's stance, the instinctive preparation to fast and violent action. He stared at Sam, his eyes slitted, waiting for him to either back down or draw.

And Sam knew that he dared do neither.

To back down would be to brand him a coward, a big-mouth, a dirty yellow-belly, and his mission demanded that he acquire a reputation for toughness. Quantrill, if he ever located him, would have no time for cowards. But to draw was to risk immediate death. Sam had no illusions as to his prowess with a six-gun. He was a good shot and could hit his target but he was nowhere near the class of men who had grown up with a gun on their hip. His years as a soldier had not helped and he knew that, if he reached for his gun, he would be dead before it cleared leather.

'I'm waiting,' said the whip-like man.

'I don't aim to kill you,' said Sam softly, and reached for the full glass he had left on the bar. He poised it in his right hand, his eyes steady as he stared at the gunman.

'Then eat crow.' The man relaxed a little, a thin smile curving the corners of his mouth and, for a split second, his eyes left Sam and drifted around the watching men. He was boastful, a little pleased that Sam had backed down, and inclined to make the most of it. He relaxed even more.

'A yellow-belly,' he sneered. 'I thought so. Just a big-mouthed wind-bag.' He looked at Sam.

Sam threw the glass of whiskey directly into his eyes.

Immediately the glass left his hand Sam was on the move. He ducked, lunging forward and, as the gunman yelled with rage and reached for his gun, Sam came upright in a smooth arcing curve. His left hand knocked aside the Colt and lead dug its way into the floor. His right fist drove against the thin jaw, his left hand gripped the other's gun, twisted, and flung the weapon to one side. He stepped back, smiling at the man before him.

He could have killed him then, whipped out his own gun and sent lead into the gunman standing before him, but to do that would be to shoot an unarmed man and, rough though the ways of the West were, yet men lived by their own code. An armed man did not draw on, or kill, an unarmed one. Sam knew that, knew too that if he tried to break the code he would be fair game for anyone with an itching trigger-finger. He was a stranger in town, the whip-like man was not, and it was inconceivable that they would permit wanton murder.

He smiled wider, dropped his hand to his belt, and drew his Colt.

'Still want me to eat my words?'

'I stick by what I said,' snapped the whip-like man. He looked at the gun in Sam's first. 'Kill me if you want to, but that don't make you right.'

'No.' Sam tossed the pistol on to the long bar. 'I said that I didn't aim to kill you, but I don't stand your kind of talk from anyone. Let's see how good you are without a gun.'

The whip-like man stared, glanced about him then, with a sudden rush, lunged at Sam. His fists hammered on the other's protecting arms, his boots kicked and his knees jabbed towards Sam's body. It was dirty fighting, all-in fighting, but Sam had expected it and the attack did not catch him unprepared.

He weaved, dodging the lashing boots and, waiting his chance, sent hammering blows to the face of the other man. He followed them, driving his blows into the stomach, the neck, slamming with all the force of his back and arm muscles, using skill and calculation to end the fight as quickly as he could.

A fist thudded against his jaw, a boot crashed against his shin and pain welled from the bruised bone. Sam gasped, staggered back, then dodged as his opponent rushed at him. He struck, sending the other man hard against the bar then, as he saw the whip-like man reach for the gun he had discarded, he dived forward and, with one long, vicious uppercut, ended the fight.

He stared sombrely down at the

figure slumped on the rough boards, shook his head, replaced his gun in its holster and, picking up the one owned by the unconscious man, opened the side-gate and spilled the cartridges into his hand. Stooping he slid the gun into its holster, threw the bullets into the street and returned to his whiskey.

'A fist fight!' The old prospector chuckled as he edged nearer. 'I ain't seen a man whipped by a pair of fists for a long time now.' He nodded his thanks as Sam slid the bottle towards him. 'Once they always used to stand up and fight like that. I've seen men beaten so that they could hardly move and still be at work the next morning.' He drank and wiped his beard. 'They don't seem to breed the same kind of man now. What with bowies and six-guns and drawing at the drop of a hat. The West ain't what it used to be.'

'Know him?' Sam glanced at the man on the floor.

'Hyram? Sure, I know him.'

'What kind of man is he?'

'Tough,' said the old man. 'Not as tough as some I've known, but a mean coyote just the same. He fancies himself as a gunslinger, had a run with the Mexicans a while ago and then almost lost his hair to the Apaches.' The old man helped himself to more whiskey. 'He ain't as mean as some though. He won't bushwhack you if that's what you're afeard of. He'll come after you and make you draw but he'll meet you face to face.'

'Sure of that?'

'As sure as I am of anything. I've known Hyram since he was a boy and he may be wild and mean but he ain't all bad.'

Sam nodded, relieved at what the old man had told him. He was not a man to be afraid of anything but he was on duty and his assignment came before any troublesome personal quarrels. He did not hate Hyram and didn't want to have to kill him. If what the old man had said was true then their quarrel could be forgotten. He reached for the bottle.

'Was he talking horse sense or was he shooting the breeze?'

'You mean about Quantrill?'

'Yes.'

'How would I know?' The old prospector stared at Sam, with shrewd eyes. 'Me, I just aim to wander around and pan a little dust. Quantrill don't bother me none and I don't aim to bother him.'

'And Hyram?'

'He's young and wild and maybe he would like to join up with Quantrill and grab himself some fun.' The old man shook his head. 'I don't know what things are coming to,' he complained. 'In my young days we didn't have no truck with wild goings on. We had the Indians to worry about, and water, and trying to get a living off the desert. Things have got too easy now, that's what it is. Store clothes and stage coaches, fancy guns and fast horses. A man gets so that he can't be alone no more. Leastways, he has to try and be alone instead of the other way about.'

'What do you think of Quantrill?'

'Me!' The old man shrugged and helped himself to more whiskey. 'I don't aim to think about it one way or another. It's like the war, it don't concern me. I'm a Westerner myself, always have been, and I don't go for fancy words or fancy clothes. Give me a mule, a sack of beans, some bacon, salt and a few bottles of whiskey and I'm satisfied. The rest of the mule-heads can fight themselves to a standstill for all I care.'

Sam nodded, recognizing the indifference of the West, the conviction that they were sufficient to themselves and able to make their own life without interference from the more civilized eastern states. He stared down as Hyram stirred.

'Feeling better?'

'Go to hell.' The whip-like man sat up, felt his jaw, then climbed slowly to his feet. Sam pushed his glass towards him and, after a second's hesitation, Hyram drank. He touched the gun in his belt and looked surprised. He checked it and stared at Sam.

'I still aim to get even.'

'I'll stand up to you any time,' said Sam. 'But not with six-guns.' He smiled at Hyram. 'I reckon a man should know when he hasn't got a chance. You could give me aces and still beat me to the draw. If you want to shoot it out we'll do it my way, guns in hand at twenty paces and fire on the drop of a hat.'

'A duel,' chuckled the old-timer. 'I seen one like that in New Orleans once. Two young Creole bucks had a grievance and they fought it out. They took pistols, we didn't have six-guns then, and stood back to back. Someone called the word and they walked away from each other, turned and fired.' He chuckled again. 'Funniest thing I ever did see.'

'What happened?' said Hyram.

'One of them got a ball between the eyes and the other collected it in the stomach. If it hadn't been for the heat they could have had a double burying but the man who got himself gut-shot took his time about handing in his chips!'

'They fought a lot in New Orleans, didn't they?' Hyram helped himself to whiskey. He seemed to have forgotten his grievance.

'They sure did,' said the old prospector. 'They used to fight with knives and swords as well as pistols. One trick they had was for a couple of knife-fighters to stand face to face, each with one boot nailed to the floor so that they couldn't run. Then they'd set about each other with a couple of big bowies, fighting until one or the other got killed or gave up. They didn't use to give up and more often than not they'd cut each other to pieces!' He sucked in his cheeks as he thought about it. 'They used to sell tickets at some of the fights and bets would be laid on the result, but they weren't the high-born Creoles fighting then, usually a couple of niggers would be set against each other, worn-out fieldhands or young bucks who had done something wrong.'

'Nice people,' said Sam. Hyram grunted, finished his drink, then looked at Sam.

'I haven't forgotten what you said,' he reminded. 'But I'm willing to let it go at that if you are.' He rubbed his jaw. 'You sure pack a mean wallop for a man who don't look so much.'

'Luck,' said Sam. He held out his hand. 'Maybe we'll meet up sometime.'

'Maybe.' Hyram shook hands, grinned, and swung through the batwing doors into the street. Sam saw him reload his pistol, mount his horse, then ride off in a cloud of dust.

Sam watched him go, sighed, then felt the old prospector tug at his sleeve.

'We was talking about grub-stakes, mister,' he said. 'You still interested?'

'No more than before,' said Sam. 'I didn't go for it then and I don't now.'

'You're missing out,' warned the old-timer. 'I ain't no big-mouth and I know where to find the pay-dirt. I can pan as much as twenty dollars a day in fine dust from some of them hills, and that's not counting the nuggets. A smart man would invest a few hundred dollars in a deal like that.'

'Maybe I'm not smart,' said Sam.

'You're smart enough,' flattered the prospector. 'You seem a man with an eye for a good thing. I tell you that if you stake me you just can't go wrong.'

'I'm no greenhorn,' said Sam, who was getting tired of the conversation. 'You could put all the gold in these parts in the corner of your eye and you wouldn't even blink. Quit wasting my time.'

'If you ain't a greenhorn then you should know better.' The old prospector seemed really annoyed. 'I can get dust off Boot-top and Horse Head, Sugar Loaf and Ranthorne, Cauldis and . . . '

'What are they, towns?' Sam had pricked up his ears at the sound of a familiar name.

'Towns? Hell no! They're hills.'

'I see.' Sam looked thoughtful. 'Which is nearest to us now?'

'Boot-top ain't so far and Ranthorne's a bit further east.'

'Funny name for a hill, isn't it?' Sam forced himself to remain indifferent. 'Who was Ranthorne?'

'It ain't named after a man,' snapped the prospector curtly. 'There are a couple of peaks which sweep up like the horns on a he-sheep. That's how it got its name.'

Sam nodded, it was logical and probably correct. Names soon became shortened and distorted with continual use and a pair of peaks originally known as the Ram's Horns would soon become known as Ranthorne. Such a place wouldn't be found on most maps, certainly not unless it was a large-scale local one. Sam felt that he was getting somewhere at last.

'I'm interested,' he said. 'Is that where you aim to get the dust?'

'No. Ranthorne's been worked out for the easy pickings. I'd head for

Boot-top or Horse Head.'

Sam nodded. 'This Ranthorne, what's the nearest town?'

'There ain't what you'd call a regular town within fifty miles,' said the old man. 'There's a place called Morgan's Forge. They have a post-house, a depot, a store and a saloon. It ain't much.'

'How far from the hill?'

'Ten, twelve miles. Why?'

'Maybe I'll take a look in that part and see if I can spot some pay dirt.' Sam smiled at the old man's expression. 'Quit worrying, old-timer, you've talked me into it. I'll stake you up to a couple of hundred dollars. That should last you a couple of months. We meet back here at the end of that time. Agreed?'

'It ain't much,' said the prospector.

'It's all I've got.'

'You've made yourself a deal. I'll strike west and cover the old ground. I'll pan the streams and take a look at a place I know of. Two months should about do it, a week maybe either way. If

I ain't here when you call in I'll leave word at the livery stable. That suit you?'

'I reckon so.' Sam knew the old man, despite his eagerness, would play fair. He would buy his goods and wander towards the west on his eternal search for gold. Maybe he would die out there, bitten by a rattler or perish from thirst or hunger. Perhaps human enemies would find him, the Apaches, and then he would leave his bones to whiten on the desert sand. If he lived he would keep his word, returning at the end of two months to share what gold he had found and to dissolve the partnership. He, like most true sons of the West, considered his word his bond.

Sam, counted out a heap of bills, all greenbacks, and smiled at the old man's expression. 'Confederate money ain't no good no more. This stuff is as good as gold dust and a sight less heavy to carry.' He put away the rest of his money. 'This Ranthorne, how would I get to it from here?'

'Head north-east for a couple of

days. That will get you to Morgan's Forge and you can spot Ranthorne from there. You'll be wasting your time though, that heap of rock has been worked out for the next five years. Then maybe the weather will have washed more dust down to the creek and it'd be worth taking another look.'

'I'll think about it,' said Sam easily. He stretched, paid for his drinks, and headed towards the door. 'See you in a couple of months, old-timer.'

The old prospector nodded, his eyes reflecting his contentment now that he had a grub-stake and could continue his search for the yellow metal. Sam grinned, left the saloon, mounted his horse and rode down the trail towards the north-east.

After a few miles he waited and then, a long time after, Leman joined him.

Together they rode towards Morgan's Forge and the place known as Ranthorne.

8

Jud sat with Quantrill in his cabin and looked at the rifle in his hands. It was one of the Winchesters they had taken from the escort and Jud, for the dozenth time, ran his hands over the smooth stock, operated the loading lever, and tested the feel and balance of the weapon.

'Repeaters,' he said. 'If we'd had these we'd have won the war.'

'We can still win it,' said Quantrill. He reached over and picked up a similar weapon. 'We can buy some of these and arm our men. We can recruit new riders and pay them standard wages. We can harry the north until they break.'

'Dreams,' said Jud. 'The war is over, Quantrill. It's over and we lost and that's all there is to it. What's the point of keeping up the conflict? We can't win. We can never win.'

'I'm not talking about winning,' snapped the small man. 'I'm talking about revenge, about refusing to admit defeat, about keeping the Stars and Bars flying in one spot of this country even if it's only here in Ranthorne. Damn it, Jud, from the way you talk a man would think that you just didn't care.'

'I care enough,' said Jud. 'Maybe I care too much. I had a family, remember?'

'I haven't forgotten,' said Quantrill. 'The last news you had was that your brother had died in a field hospital, that your parents had perished in the burning of your house, that you have nothing to return to. Nothing at all.' Quantrill sighed. 'Sherman didn't leave much behind him on his march through Georgia. The mansions burned and looted, the slaves freed, crippling taxes applied to all owners of land so that they had to surrender them to the carpetbaggers. If we can believe half of what we hear the South must be a living hell for those who returned from the war.'

'I know it.'

'Then you know how I feel.' Quantrill took up the rifle again. 'New weapons, Jud. New men, restless riders who will jump at the chance to strike a blow for the Cause. General Lee may have signed the peace but I haven't and I'm not going to. While I live the Confederacy lives with me and every Yankee is my enemy.'

His eyes blazed as he thought about it, the sallow skin of his cheeks flushing and accentuating the Spanish blood which ran in his veins. Staring at him Jud recognized him for what he was, a fanatic, a man lost in a dream, the dream of the Southern Cause, and he knew that Quantrill would fight until he died.

And he would ride with Quantrill.

It was inertia that did it, that and the fact that for four years now he had lived, rode, ate, talked and breathed the same air, the same food as Quantrill. The man's fanaticism was catching and it was hard to shake off the convictions of four years. They had been four years of ruthless conflict, legal conflict, and the habit had become almost a part of him. Part of him told him to stop, that the war was over, that now there was no enemy to fight. But another part remembered the ruin of the South, the endless fighting for an ideal, and that part refused to admit that all the dead, the struggle, the loss of pride and the hardship had been for nothing.

It was easier to listen to Quantrill, to agree with his warped logic, to ride and kill and risk a clean and sudden death, to follow the old, familiar pattern instead of turning over a new page and starting life all over again.

'We are increasing our numbers almost every day,' said Quantrill. 'Brenhardt is passing the word along the border and men are riding to join us. Soon we will be back at our old strength and then, with that amount of men, we can ride deep into the North.'

'When?' Jud was tired of sitting doing nothing. He craved for action, swift and violent action, in which he would have no time to think or ponder the future. The raid which had won them a million dollars in greenbacks was several weeks old. It had been a time of waiting and of sending out messengers to gather information. They had returned, those messengers, with grim stories of atrocities done by the victorious Northern armies, of freed slaves wandering the deserted fields, starving while their liberators laughed and passed them by. The chivalry of the South was dead, the great plantations broken, the grand mansions burned, the entire Confederacy thrown into chaos.

Many men who had thought themselves rich were now beggars as the money they had had, the Confederate money, lost its value and became worthless. Only gold and silver and greenbacks had any value now, and only the Northern businessmen, the vote-catching carpetbaggers, and the rising politicians had any real money. They paid their own price for land worth a thousand times the value they set on it. They took what they wanted, used their own elected officers to enforce crippling laws, and reduced the proud South to abject poverty.

It would pass as all things pass. Things would level themselves and a measure of prosperity return to the cottonlands, but all that was in the future and to Jud and those like him, it was as if his entire life had suddenly fallen away from him leaving him naked and helpless in the aftermath of war.

And so they clung to the one certain thing they knew. They clung to the man who had led and guided them for four long years. They clung to Quantrill with a dog-like devotion, sharing his hate, his desperation, riding with him as they had always done because it was the one thing they knew how to do.

And now it was time to strike again.

'We need money,' said Quantrill. 'We need millions in gold and greenbacks. With money we can do anything, bribe our spies, buy guns, hire men, get horses and food. We can help the South with gold and dollars more than we can by crippling the Northern war effort. Blowing up trains and arsenals will not help us now. We must go after money, money all the time, and with it we can pour a stream of aid into the South and help to repair some of the damage.'

His eyes glistened as he looked into the future.

'Think of it, Jud. We shall never be beaten. We shall give gold to those who need it, the crippled veteran, the dispossessed landowners, the starving and the sick. We shall act as an invisible army, punishing wrong and bolstering the weak. The carpetbaggers will learn to fear us. The slaves will recognize us as their natural masters, the beaten armies will rally to us. In five years, ten, we shall be strong enough to ride North and beat the Yankees to their knees. I tell you, Jud, that the South is not really beaten. We are suffering a temporary defeat and, when the hour is ripe, we shall strike and win a deciding victory.'

He paused and his cheeks glowed with colour as he fed his ambition with words and thoughts stemming from dreams.

'We can afford to wait, Jud. We shall build up a great war-chest and rally soldiers to our cause. In ten years the North will have grown careless but we shall have grown strong. We shall recruit men, train them, and ship them North to wait for the hour. They can go up the Mississippi to St Louis, to Iowa, to Minnesota. We can pour an army into Northern territory and, at the same time, build a combat force in Mexico, paid with Yankee gold. We shall wait until all is ready and then . . . ' His hands smashed hard on the wooden table. 'The North will be ours!'

'Words,' said Jud, his eyes gleaming at the picture Quantrill had painted. 'Just words. When do we start?'

'As soon as Brenhardt gets back. He is bringing in some new men. When he arrives we take the men that are here and head north to Memphis.'

'To Memphis?'

'They have opened a businessmen's bank there,' said Quantrill grimly. 'We'll rob it and swing back here.'

'Memphis is a garrison town,' said Jud thoughtfully. 'Our last raid cost us nine men. Count the smith, the cook, the guards and the wounded, and we won't have more than ten men able to ride with us. It isn't enough.'

'We can take the guards, Brenhardt's men can stand watch.'

'No.' Jud was positive in his denial. 'If we lose Ranthorne we lose everything. Aside from that I wouldn't trust those men with the money we have here. I say leave a strong guard of men we can trust. We can take some of the new men with us to make up our numbers. How many do you plan on taking?'

'At least twenty. We'll have to leave some outside town to cover our get-away. The rest of us will enter town and split up. Some will cover the street while the rest of us rob the bank. It will have to be a daylight raid so speed and timing are essential.'

'The more men we have the better,' said Jud. 'We can plant them in town to run interference and if they call for a posse they can volunteer so as to throw off the pursuit.' He rose from the table as a man shouted from outside and the clatter of hooves filled the clearing. 'Brenhardt. Let's see what luck he had.'

Quantrill nodded and followed the tall man from the cabin.

Brenhardt had returned with a score of men, all tough, hard-faced, almost criminal-looking men. All were well-armed, many with the new Winchesters, and all with six-guns hanging low on their hips. They stared at Quantrill with insolent appraisal and, in turn, he stared back.

'A tough bunch of rannies,' said Brenhardt as he dismounted. 'I collected most of them from across the border and the rest from the fly-towns down south. Maybe they ain't as gentlemanly as officer types but they can ride and shoot and all have a yearning to live easy.' He chuckled. 'Show these boys a bank or a stagecoach and they'll tear it apart with their bare hands.'

Quantrill nodded, his face masking his inner feelings. He stared at the men, his eyes slipping from face to face as if seeking for a familiar person.

Sam Wayland forced himself to meet that stare with insolent casualness.

It had been sheer luck his managing to tie up with Brenhardt. The sort of luck which a man makes for himself if he tries hard and long enough. In part he owed it to Hyram, in part to his own willingness to take a risk. Sam himself had ridden as close as he dared to Ranthorne and then, just as he was trying to think of a way to join Quantrill without getting himself shot first, he had ridden into Brenhardt and a bunch of men. Luck had been with him then for one of the men had been Hyram, the whip-like man he had fought and beaten back in the little town. Hyram had recognized him and, so pleased had he been at riding to join Quantrill, that he had recommended Sam as a man handy with his fists and gun. That recommendation, together with Sam's own fast talking, had calmed Brenhardt's fears. The squat man was eager to gather as many new riders as possible and he had accepted Sam at his face valuation, inviting him to join up with the bunch.

Now Sam was in Ranthorne, face to face with Quantrill, the man he had sworn to destroy.

'You know who I am,' snapped Quantrill. 'And you know what I stand for. If you want to ride with me you must obey my orders and those of my Captains.' He looked at Jud and Brenhardt. 'Now, all of you raise your right hand and repeat after me. I swear by Almighty God that . . . '

The rolling words of the oath echoed

from the rock walls of the clearing and the answer, mumbled for the most part, sounded like the distant washing of a turbulent sea.

'You are now enlisted into the army of the Confederate States,' said Quantrill. 'You will fight and conduct yourselves as soldiers. As we have no facilities here for punishment I warn you now. Disobedience will result in death. Any questions?'

'When do we eat?'

'Later.' Quantrill glanced up at the sky. 'At sundown.'

'When do we get our hands on some money?'

'All in good time.' Quantrill gestured towards the corral. 'Unsaddle your horses, take your gear into the cabins, and stand by. I will instruct you later on your duties!' He hesitated. 'Do any of you know Memphis at all?

'I do,' said Sam. He grinned. 'I holed out there a couple of weeks a few years back.'

'More recent knowledge?'

'Sure, I passed through maybe a month ago.' He shrugged. 'I hardly knew the place, it's springing up like grass after a rain.'

'Report now to the cabin,' snapped Quantrill. 'Brenhardt, follow me. Jud, join us as soon as you are able.'

Sam nodded and spurred his horse towards the corral. He unsaddled, turned his horse after the others, and picking up his gear went into one of the cabins. Hyram waved to him and Sam set his bedroll on the bunk next to the one the whip-like man was occupying.

'What's Quantrill want you for, Sam?'

'Search me.' Sam hung his rifle on a peg and dumped his saddle beneath the bunk. He stretched. 'Hell, but I'm tired. I guess that maybe I'll take a walk to ease my bones.'

'Better see Quantrill first,' warned Hyram. 'That man's sure dynamite. You hear what he said about killing anyone who didn't jump when he said so?'

'I heard him.'

'Think he means it?'

'Maybe.' Sam grinned as he eased the pistol at his belt. 'I figure that it'd take more than a half-pint to teach me tricks.'

'He's a mean man, Sam.'

'I'll remember it,' said Sam. He grinned. 'Be seeing you — soldier.' He walked out of the cabin.

He found all three officers in the cabin. They were staring at a map of Memphis as Sam entered and Quantrill gestured to the yellowed paper.

'How up-to-date is this map?'

'Most of it is accurate,' said Sam as he stared at it. 'But the town's grown some since they drew that thing.' He rested his finger on the paper. 'There's a livery stable there and a store there. They've built another couple of saloons about here and the rail-head has spread some.' His finger traced designs on the map.

'You seem to know how to read maps,' said Jud. 'Where did you learn that?'

'I was in the Militia,' said Sam easily. 'That was a long time ago before I was dry behind the ears. They showed us how to read them things.'

'In the Militia?' Quantrill glanced at Jud. 'Where?'

'Johnson's Creek down in Tennessee. My Pap moved west about six years ago, he got himself killed by the Indians, and Ma died of the fever. I've been riding around since picking up what I could where I could.'

'Did you fight in the war?'

'No.' Sam shrugged. 'I told you, I was out West, most of the time in New Mexico. We had enough to do fighting the Indians without worrying much over the rumpus back East.'

'I see.' Quantrill looked thoughtful. 'How was it you happened to be in Memphis?'

'I heard that there was pickings to be had,' said Sam. 'Some of the boys had collected a fistful of jewels and other stuff just by riding down south. I figured that I'd take a look round and see what was going.'

'A looter.' Quantrill stared his distaste. 'Did you collect anything?'

'No. I was late in the game and the chips had been cleared. I swung back north, never mind why, and holed out in Memphis.' Sam shrugged. 'I was drifting back west when I bumped into your man Brenhardt.'

'That's right,' said Brenhardt. 'He rode smack into us.'

'So you don't know him?' Jud stared at Sam. 'For all we know, this man could be a spy.'

'Watch it,' said Sam, and his face lost its easy grin. 'I don't figure on standing that talk from anyone.'

'You said that you had collected these men from over the border,' insisted Jud to Brenhardt. 'How can you vouch for this man?'

'Hyram knew him,' said Brenhardt sullenly. 'And I know Hyram. He's a good man and I stand by him. He said that this ranny was what we needed and I agreed with him.' He laughed. 'Hell, what are you afraid of? We can watch him, can't we? Anyway, what can we do about it? We take that risk with every new man we recruit.'

It was true and Jud knew it. He sighed and looked at Quantrill. 'What do you think?'

'I think that we're wasting time,' snapped the small man. 'Sam, I want you to bring this map up-to-date as far as you can. I want you to pay particular attention to the bank and the streets leading to it.'

'We going to rob the bank?'

'That's my business,' snapped Quantrill. 'You just do as you're told.'

'Now wait a minute.' Sam straightened and stared at Quantrill. 'Let's get one thing straight before we go any further. I aim to ride with you, yes, but I'm no dog. I want to know what I'm doing and why I'm doing it. I'm no fancy soldier to be told what to do and then get himself shot while doing it. If we're going to rob the bank then that's all right, but I want to know and I want my share. Start coming the high horse with me, mister, and one of us is going to be awfully sorry.'

Quantrill didn't answer but his eyes, as he stared at the young man, burned with naked fury. He rose, his hand dropping to his pistol and Sam tensed himself for coming action.

'Take it easy,' said Brenhardt. He stepped forward between the two men. 'Don't let's start shooting each other.' He grinned at Quantrill. 'I told you that these rannies were tough and hard. They'll ride and fight for us but as equals, not as underlings.'

'They are soldiers of the Confederate Army,' said Quantrill.

'Maybe so,' agreed Brenhardt, 'but let 'em get used to the idea.' He turned to Sam and winked. 'Back down, ranny, and give the boss his head. If you want to dip your fingers in gold dust follow Quantrill. Punching holes in each other won't get you any of the folding money that's waiting to be picked up.' He winked again, significantly, and Sam shrugged.

'I'll play the game your way,' he said. 'Just so's we understand each other!'

'We understand,' said Brenhardt quickly. 'Now how about that map?'

Sam grunted and stooped over the paper. He picked up a pencil and drew on the map. He added buildings, drew in streets and made it as accurate as his memory allowed.

'Thank you,' said Quantrill coldly. 'That will be all for now. I suggest that you get some rest, we will be riding soon.'

'When?'

'Maybe tomorrow,' stepped in Brenhardt before Quantrill could answer. He took Sam's arm and led him out of the cabin. They walked for a while in silence then the squat man halted and looked around to make sure that they were out of earshot.

'Bear down, Sam,' he warned. 'Quantrill ain't a man to take that kind of talk from no one. He don't care what he does either. You're liable to get a slug between the shoulders if he feels that way.'

'Hyram told me that we was to get plenty of pickings,' said Sam. 'It don't seem that way to me.'

'It will do,' soothed Brenhardt. 'You just ride with me and you'll be neck-deep in greenbacks before you know it.' He sucked in his breath. 'Quantrill's a mite gone in the head but you needn't worry about that. Just stand by me and everything will be Jake.' He stared at Sam. 'You look a smart fellow and I don't have to draw a picture. Sometimes a man's got to figure things out for himself. Get me?'

'I get you,' said Sam. He grinned. 'Count on me, Brenhardt, you and me talk the same language.'

'That's the idea.' The squat man slapped Sam on the shoulder. 'Keep a rein on your tongue, son, and grab yourself some sack-time. When we ride there won't be time for shut-eye.'

He winked and returned to the cabin to confer with Jud and Quantrill. Sam, his mind busy with what he had learned, strolled towards the cabin where he had left his gear. Obviously Quantrill was planning a raid on Memphis and, from what he had said, the bank was the objective. Unless the military were warned it was highly possible that the riders would get away with it. There would be shooting and killing of innocent people. The bank would be gutted and the depositors ruined. Quantrill, for some reason of his own, had turned bankrobber and, to Sam's way of thinking, that made him no better than a common outlaw.

He had to be stopped and stopped fast.

Sam tilted his head and stared up at the sky. The sun was setting and the floor of the clearing was in shadow. Up higher the twin peaks were still illuminated by the sun and, staring at them, Sam decided to risk what he had in mind.

From his gear he took a small shaving mirror, slipped it in his pocket, and left the cabin. Outside the new arrivals lounged or indulged in horse play, some were shooting at targets and a few were busy at a poker game. Most of them had drifted all over the clearing and Sam, as he strolled towards the pass, caused no comment. He walked slowly down the pass until he was hidden from the clearing. As far as he knew all the guards would be staring outwards towards the foothills but, even so, he decided to take a chance. Reaching for a spur of rock he began to climb the peak, swinging and clawing his way upwards until the full light of the setting sun shone in his face.

Below him, a dark figure against the rocks, he could see the shape of one of the guards and others, he knew, were scattered about the pass. He hoped that none of them would turn at the wrong moment.

He took the shaving mirror from his pocket and, holding it so that it reflected the sun, began to move it with careful deliberation. His message was simple, spelled out in morse code and consisted of one word repeated over and over for as long as he dared.

'Memphis,' he signalled. 'M — E — M — P — H — I — S.' Twenty times he flashed the signal, using the shaving mirror as an improvized heliograph, then, putting away the mirror, he began the difficult descent. Luck was with him again and he reached the pass without being discovered. He was walking towards the clearing when Jud approached him.

'Where have you been?'

'Just down the pass a piece.' Sam stared at the tall man with calm insolence. 'Just killing the time until chow.'

'Chow is ready,' said Jud. 'Better get it while it's going.'

He stared after Sam as he walked towards the cook fires, now glowing in the dusk. Thoughtfully he stared up at the peaks, still painted with the red and gold, pink and orange beauty of the setting sun.

His face, as he continued down the pass to check the guards, was very thoughtful.

9

They rode at midnight, twenty men together with Jud and Quantrill, each man leading a spare horse, all armed with revolvers and the new Winchester rifles. The party was half-and-half of old riders and new, the new ones including both Hyram and Sam. Brenhardt, together with the rest of the men, had been left behind to guard Ranthorne and to await the arrival of a score of fresh recruits.

They rode in silence, intent on covering as much ground as possible before daylight, pausing only to change horses so as to give the burdened beasts a rest. At dawn they camped, setting guards and eating cold, sleeping and checking their weapons as they waited for the sun to crawl across the sky and night to come to shield their movements from any casual watcher.

Night came and once again they rode like men possessed, spurring their mounts and not stopping for food or rest, only to change horses and once, for almost an hour, while Quantrill sent out scouts to report on the terrain. Day came and again they rested, their stomachs cramped from the cold beans and bacon. Quantrill passed out a jug of whiskey and the soaked pieces of corn bread in the potent spirit, chewing them as they lay in the sun.

'Fast travel,' said Hyram to Sam. 'Even with stopping all day we're still covering plenty of territory. Wonder when we'll get there?'

'Tomorrow, I guess,' said Sam. He was worried. Quantrill had started out sooner than he had expected and, even if Leman had caught his signal, there would be little time for him to contact the military and have troops posted to Memphis. That was assuming he had caught the signal at all. He could have been relaxed and missed the brief flashes. Sam hoped that his companion had stayed on the job.

Hyram grunted and sucked at his whiskey-soaked bread.

'When this is over,' he said, 'I'm taking my share of the loot and having myself a spree in a little town I know, south of the border. Fried chicken, tequila, tamales and a nice, dark-haired beauty to serve it. Wine and music and a hot game of poker.' He chuckled. 'Come easy go easy, that's the way to live.'

'Maybe Quantrill's got different ideas,' said Sam. 'Maybe he doesn't reckon on splitting the loot. You're a soldier now, don't forget, and soldiers work for pay.'

'Not this soldier.' Hyram grinned. 'Don't you worry, Sam, everything'll turn out just Jake. We've got Brenhardt on our side and he's not a man to sit on a pile of gold while his throat aches for whiskey. Play along with Brenhardt and you'll have no regrets.' He raised himself and stared to where Quantrill sat talking to Jud. 'Quantrill's gone sour in the head, Sam. He may enjoy working for glory but this child's working for his own pockets.'

'Does Quantrill know that?'

'He will,' said Hyram and chuckled again. 'He will.'

'Maybe he won't like it?'

'That's his grief,' Hyram grunted and lit a cigar. 'Every man's got to lean sometime, Sam, and maybe it's Quantrill's turn to take a few orders instead of giving them.' He stared at the small man. 'Look at him, sitting there like a turkey cock. I wonder what he's talking about?'

Quantrill was talking about Memphis.

'You will ride in ahead of me with half of the men,' he said. 'Position yourselves in the streets ready to block pursuit. I will arrive at mid-day, head directly for the bank and rob it of all it contains. There will probably be some shooting, that cannot be helped.'

'Shooting civilians is different to fighting the military,' said Jud slowly.

'No different,' said Quantrill. 'They

are all the enemy and besides, how can we avoid it?' He shook his head.

'Which men will you take?' asked Jud. 'The old or the new riders?'

'We will mix them. The new men need the touch of discipline and I cannot rely on them as I can on our old comrades.' Quantrill looked thoughtful. 'They are expendable. Some of them have peculiar ideas and may cause trouble. See to it that they are not allowed to form a group of their own. The old riders will carry the money and the new can be used to beat off the opposition.'

'And after the action?'

'We rendezvous here if separated, but I do not think that we will. The best plan would be to unite at the edge of town and make a quick journey towards Ranthorne. We can throw off or destroy pursuit if it comes too close!' Quantrill shrugged. 'Speed is our main weapon. Speed and quick shooting.' He glanced at the setting sun. 'Gather the men, we start as soon as the sun is below the horizon.'

That night they rode at a more leisurely pace, conserving their strength for the action to come. A few miles from Memphis the spare horses were left together with two men to act as guards and the main body pressed on. Closer to the town Jud and ten men rode forward and mingled with the crowds in the growing city. They hitched their horses to the rails running along the boardwalk, spread so as to cover the approaches to the bank, and sat or lounged, their eyes watchful, while half of their number at a time caught themselves a meal or a drink.

There was a reason for that. Jud knew that a moving man was not a suspicious one, but that any group who sat for hours for no apparent reason would be immediately suspect. He himself roved around the town, his eyes and ears open, his nerves tensed for anything out of the ordinary. As the climbing sun reached towards high noon he returned to his position at the hitching rail, letting his eyes drift over his men, all casual, all with their eyes looking for trouble, all ready to explode into violent action should it be necessary.

Noon came and, with it, Quantrill.

He rode at the head of his men, the reins loose in his hands and his body casual and devoid of strain. Behind him, straggled out as if they had happened together by mere chance, the rest of his men followed. Quantrill dismounted at the bank, hitching his horse to the rail and, while he was lighting a cigar, others joined him. The cigar lit to his satisfaction Quantrill entered the bank, the doors swung behind him, and he stared at the clerk behind the counter.

'Good-day, sir,' said the young man. He smiled. He wore a store suit of black broadcloth, his hair shone with grease and his face was pallid from too long indoors. Other men were in the bank, a couple of depositors, three clerks and an old man who dozed over a shotgun. Behind the counter through thick doors, Quantrill could see the bars of a vault. He approached the counter.

'I want to make a deposit,' he said. Out of the corner of his eye he could see that two of his men had entered the bank and were leaning against the far wall. They seemed to be waiting their turn at the counter. The doors opened again, shut, and a hard voice rapped commands.

'Raise your hands! Fast! If anyone moves I'll plug him!'

The old man grunted, stared, and went for his shotgun.

Jud swore as the sound of shots came from the bank. The one thing both he and Quantrill had hoped for was that the robbery could be done in silence. Gunshots were the surest way of telling the people that something was wrong. A fresh burst of firing came from the bank and, in the following silence, men's voices could be heard as they called to each other asking what was wrong. Several moved towards the bank, their hands grabbing at their hips and, as they moved, Jud yelled and swung into the saddle. He rode towards the bank, yelling and blasting the air with his six-gun, riding past and reining to reload. After him came two of his men, the rest remaining at their posts.

For a moment it seemed that his ruse would succeed, that the people would blame all the shots on to him, a supposedly drunken cowboy, then a man yelled to another and both advanced towards the bank.

Guns flared and they dropped where they stood.

Other guns roared their song of flame and lead and men, innocent men, spun and died beneath the storm of bullets. Jud swore as he saw what had happened, cursing the trigger-happy fools who had loosed the destruction, then stiffened as he heard an all-too-familiar sound. He dug his heels into his mount, darted down the street to an inter-section, then rode back frantically the way he had come.

After him galloped a full company of military.

Quantrill came out of the bank as Jud reached it. He stared at the tall man, then gestured to the others to mount.

'The Army,' snapped Jud. 'Here, now, we've got to ride like hell!'

'Cover us,' ordered the small man. He leapt to his saddle, the bags stuffed with bills swinging as he looped them over the saddle-horn. He turned his horse and, at full gallop, rode down the street, the other following him. Jud, his lips thinned, rode back to where he had left his men only to find that they too had ridden after Quantrill. He was alone, in a hostile town, directly in the path of the advancing soldiers!

He owed his life to the fact that they did not shoot. They held their fire for fear of hitting innocent citizens but those citizens had no such fears. Jud ducked as lead droned about him and, furiously, spurred his mount to ride after Quantrill. He crouched low in the saddle as he rode, sensing rather than feeling the lead which plucked at his clothing, his lips bared as he thought of the fiasco the raid had turned out to be.

Desperately he fumbled in his pockets, produced a fused stick of dynamite and, taking his pistol from its holster, fired directly at the tip of the fuse. The flash from the muzzle ignited the white, string-like fuse and it spluttered, shooting off a thin shower of sparks. Dropping the bomb behind him Jud rode even faster, spurring towards the cloud of dust before him which marked the passage of the men with Quantrill.

Behind him the dynamite exploded with a blast of thunder and, twisting in his saddle, he saw the main body of the cavalry in complete chaos. But ahead of them, untouched by the explosion, six men rode with grim determination.

Far ahead Quantrill managed to get his men under control and, as he heard the roar of the blast, he reined to a halt, shouting quick orders.

'Hold! Stand your ground and use

your rifles. Get those soldiers chasing Jud.'

'Jud can look after himself,' snarled one of the new riders. 'Let's get out of here.' He dug spurs into his mount, started forward, then slumped from the saddle as lead smashed his spine.

'I said hold,' snapped Quantrill. He stared at the others, the pistol smoking in his hand. 'Obey me you scum or I'll kill you myself. Get your rifles and cut down those troopers.'

It made sense, good sense, and, cowed by the pistol in Quantrill's hands, they moved to obey. They outnumbered the soldiers and were at rest. A good shot could knock a man from the saddle and, unless they did so, Quantrill knew that the pursuit would give them no time to rest or reorganise. He waited until the galloping figure of Jud had reached them then, aiming his pistol, he rapped the order to fire.

'Now!'

Three men fell at the first volley and the rest, flinging shots before them, came thundering on. Two more went down, their horses screaming as they felt the bite of lead then the remaining soldier, recognising defeat, swung his mount and galloped away.

'Let him go,' snapped Quantrill. He was very pale, and held his hand hard against his hide. 'Now mount and ride to where we left the horses. Stay together and obey orders. If you run hog-wild now none of us will ever reach safety.'

Jud lit a cigar and, satisfied it was burning well, rode next to the small man. Beneath them the trail flowed past like a black ribbon between two banks of dusty green. Ahead nothing stirred save for a few wisps of cloud in the sky. Behind them, thin in the distance, came the regular beat of horses' hooves as the soldiers, reorganised, took up the chase.

'What went wrong?' Jud dragged at his cigar, the wind taking the smoke and sending it streaming behind him.

'One of the new men lost his head and cut loose with his gun,' said

Quantrill. 'The fool shot an old man when he could have knocked him out. At the blast the others went haywire and cut down the clerks. We had to race to get any money at all and even then took only a fraction of what was in the bank. Your shots outside didn't help any.'

'Same trouble,' said Jud. 'These recruits of Brenhardt's shoot before they think.' He twisted and stared down the trail. 'That isn't the trouble, though. I don't like the fact that a company of cavalry was in town at the same time. If it hadn't been for luck they'd have caught us for certain. Maybe it was just as well that the action started before time.'

'Coincidence,' said Quantrill. 'Maybe the shots attracted them. If we had kept silent they wouldn't have come near us!'

'Maybe.' Jud didn't sound as if he believed that. 'To me they knew where they were going and they were in a hurry to get there.'

Quantrill didn't answer.

'They acted as if they knew something was due to happen,' insisted Jud. 'If we hadn't been lucky we would have been trapped. If I hadn't had that dynamite then they would have caught us by now.' He. frowned into the distance. 'If they did expect us . . . ' he said more to himself than to the small man '. . . then they would have staked the trails.' He pointed ahead. 'See that patch of shrub where it comes close to the trail?'

'I see it.' Quantrill swayed a little in his saddle. 'What of it?'

'We'd better miss it.' Jud swung his horse to the right. 'If there's an ambush waiting for us there I don't want to ride into it.'

The sound of their hooves softened as the iron struck the softer dirt to the side of the trail and their pace lessened a trifle at the heavier going. To their left the shrub came nearer, came abreast, then suddenly exploded into a charging mass of blue-uniformed men. Jud's guess had been right and the soldiers, seeing that they could no longer strike from ambush, had left their cover to chase the riders.

'Dismount!' rapped out Quantrill. 'Use rifles and knock down those horses.' He swore at the lack of obedience. 'Dismount, you fools. Those Yankees will run us down inside five miles if you try to run for it.' He slipped from his saddle, snatched his rifle, and flung himself full length on the grass. Jud, pausing only long enough to see that the others were following Quantrill's example, did likewise.

'Got any giant powder left, Jud?'

'Some.'

'Use it.'

Jud nodded and stared down the sights of his Winchester. He waited until he had a soldier on the bead, pulled the trigger, jerked the loading lever and fired again. All around him the riders were doing the same, firing their guns as fast as they could jerk the lever and press the trigger. From the huddled men a cloud of smoke rose, drifting in the slight wind.

From the advancing soldiers more smoke lifted as they returned the fire. They rode low in the saddle, their rifles spitting lead, but they presented the better targets and, as the riders aimed at the horses, the troopers toppled from their saddles to lie injured or silent in death.

'Dynamite,' snapped Quantrill. 'Now.'

Jud pulled a bomb from his pocket, touched his cigar to the fuse, and threw the small package towards the place where the soldiers crouched behind the bodies of their dead horses. Three times he repeated the action and then, when the echoes of the blast had died away, Quantrill rose to his feet and charged towards the lifting cloud of smoke, his six-gun flaming in his hand. Others followed him and, when it was all over, not one of the soldiers remained alive.

But the raiders had lost half their men in the fierce encounter.

'You're hurt!' Jud caught Quantrill as he swayed, his hand slipping from the widening patch of blood on his side. 'A stray?'

'I collected it when we stopped for you back in town,' Quantrill shrugged. 'Forget it, I'm not the only one hurt. Let's get mounted and on our way.'

'What about the wounded?' Sam, his face white from the execution he had witnessed, pointed to three riders who lay groaning on the grass. Sam hated the riders for what they had done and what they stood for and yet he had to carry out his assignment to the end. So far he had shot wild, making plenty of noise but doing no damage. Despite this he stood to be shot by anyone riding against Quantrill and, if caught, he would probably be killed out of hand before he could prove his identity.

'If they can ride we'll take them with us,' said Quantrill. 'If not . . . '

'You'd leave them here?'

'To talk?' Quantrill shook his head, his face twisted with the pain of his own wound. 'They come with us or they die.'

'I see.' Sam swallowed and went to help the wounded men into the saddle. Hyram was one of them, his face grey with the pain of a shattered leg, and he leaned heavily on Sam as the young man rode beside him.

'He meant it,' said Hyram. 'That sidewinder would have shot us to stop us talking.' He gritted his teeth as his mount galloped forward. 'Hell! If we get out of this mess I'll have something to say to Quantrill.'

'Save your breath,' snapped Sam shortly. 'You'll need it.'

Two hours' fast riding brought them to where the spare horses were waiting and they changed mounts, explaining to the two men who had served as guards just what had happened. Then, swinging wide to avoid towns and trails, they struck south, riding all the rest of the day without pause and, at sun-down, camped by the side of a little creek. They needed the rest. The horses were almost blown, lathered with sweat and trembling from fatigue. The men were in little better condition, even the unwounded among them, while the wounded groaned and whimpered from the strain of the cruel ride.

Hyram fell from his saddle and Sam caught him just in time. Quickly the young man fetched water from the creek, bathed Hyram's face and neck, then took a bottle of whiskey from his saddle-bag.

'Thanks.' The whip-like man managed to grin, then became serious. 'I'm finished, Sam. I've been losing blood all the afternoon and I'm about drained dry. I wouldn't even be able to give a gnat a decent drink.'

'You'll pull through,' said Sam, and knew as he stared at the grey features of the man that he lied. Hyram shook his head.

'I'm a goner, Sam, and I know it.' He wet his lips with the tip of his tongue. 'Listen. Trust Brenhardt. He's got a plan and he'll be waiting for us. Forget

Quantrill, Sam, he's no good. Follow Brenhardt and . . . '

He grinned — then, abruptly, his face altered, seeming to fall in on itself and, as Sam watched, he died.

Sam rose to his feet and looked around. Of the twenty men who had left Ranthorne only six were left and of those only two, he and Jud, were unwounded. Two others lay in silent heaps and two others had fallen from their saddles during the wild, non-stop ride. Near to him a man cursed as he dressed his shoulder and another, his hands trembling, lifted a whiskey bottle to his mouth, the clicking of the neck against his teeth sounding strangely clear in the night.

'On your feet, men.' Quantrill, swaying in the moonlight, one side of his clothing from the waist down a rusty brown from dried blood, stared at the riders on the ground. 'On your feet and into the saddle. We must ride fast tonight before the cavalry manages to ring us with patrols. Another brush with them and it will be all over.'

'How are you feeling?' Jud stepped towards the small man. He had taken the opportunity during the halt to dress the wound but Quantrill had lost too much blood and Jud knew that further exertions could only have one end.

'Like hell,' said the small man. 'But I'm not dead yet and I don't aim to be. Get that money on your horse, Jud. We'll leave the dead and dying here and take their mounts as spares. Ride!'

The moonlight was very bright as they left the creek, and things seemed almost as bright as day. Only the colours were absent in the falsely bright glare so that the six men looked more like ghosts than flesh and blood riders. They pressed on, saving their horses as much as possible and, at dawn, managed to find a shelter away from casual inspection, a tiny valley buried deep in the hills. Here they rested, building a small fire to warm food for their starved stomachs and gulping at the hot coffee Jud brewed in a billy.

Sam slept a little, then relieved Jud at his post, watching for the tell-tale signs of cavalry. Once he saw a troop pass within gunshot and was tempted to signal. He resisted the temptation, the job wasn't yet finished and, even though Leman would have posted soldiers around Ranthorne, yet Sam couldn't be too certain that the Captain had received and reported his message. The fiasco at Memphis could have been sheer coincidence.

The day was warm and he must have dozed a little for he awoke to find Jud standing a few feet away staring at him. He rose and looked at the tall man.

'Everything all right?'

'No.' Jud looked worried. 'You know anything about doctoring?'

'A little, why?'

'Quantrill is bad. I think that he's dying. I've plugged and washed his wound but there's nothing else I can do. I — '

He broke off, a startled expression on his face. From the camp had come the sharp, unmistakable sound of pistol shots.

Sam was the first to reach the camp and it took but a glance to see that the three riders were dead. Quantrill, his face ghastly, sat with his back against a tree and, by his side, his long-barrelled Colt rested where it had fallen from his hand. On his shirt blood pulsed from a freshly-made wound, merging with the dried blood at his waist.

'I dozed off,' he said in a whisper. 'I woke to see those rannies raiding the saddle-bags. They were talking about taking the money and making a run for Mexico. I tried to stop them but I guess that I wasn't as fast as I thought. One of them managed to get off a shot before I cut him down!' He coughed and blood gushed from his mouth. 'I'm dying, Jud. This is the end of the line.'

'Don't try to speak,' said Jud. 'Take it easy.'

'What for?' Quantrill tried to grin. 'We've ridden together for the last time, Jud. Remember when we started? A couple of officers trying to beat the North all on our own?' He coughed again and his voice, when he spoke, was choked and strangling with warm wetness.

'Would have done it too if it hadn't been for Brenhardt's men. They're no good, Jud. They aren't interested in the Cause. Must have been crazy to trust them — to trust Brenhardt — money is all he wants — I — '

'Quantrill!'

'I can hear you, Jud.' Quantrill tried to raise himself from the tree. 'Don't let Brenhardt — '

He coughed again, blood staining his shirt and chin. He lifted his hand as if to wipe his beard, looked at it, then sighed.

He died with the falling of his hand.

10

There were no troops around Ranthorne. Sam followed Jud as he wended his way towards the pass and, with every step of the tired horses, he expected soldiers to challenge them. No challenge came and Sam felt the bleakness of despair as he realized what must have happened. Leman, even if he had received the signal, had not understood it. Or perhaps he hadn't received it at all and the fiasco at Memphis was due to coincidence. Or again, the failure to surround the hills was due to lack of a good liaison in the higher command. Whatever the reason the stronghold of the raiders was free from attack.

Jud rode silently, his head bent in deep thought. The death of Quantrill had shaken him more than he cared to admit. They had been together for too long, he had absorbed some of the small man's fanaticism, and now that he was dead Jud felt that he had lost a part of himself. He straightened as they entered the pass.

'Home, Sam,' he said. 'It feels good to be back.'

Sam nodded, not replying. He felt as if he were riding into a trap for, as far as he was concerned, all his labour had gone for nothing. Even if Leman had received the message all it had accomplished was the death of the raiding party which had attacked Memphis. Even that victory had proved barren because the raiders had killed more than double their number. Silently he followed the tall man along the pass and into the clearing.

Jud frowned as he rode, glancing up at the twin peaks as if expecting something to happen. Sam could guess what it was. There should be guards stationed on those rocky heights, guards to challenge anyone riding down the pass, and no challenge had come.

Either there were no guards or they had recognized the riders and let them pass in silence.

Even Sam did not guess the truth.

He heard Jud curse as they rode into the clearing and then, as he saw what lay before them, he felt his own anger mounting.

A great fire blazed in the centre of the camp and men, reeling and staggering, moved around it. Each man was armed, ready to ride, and each held a bottle in one hand. Brenhardt, his broad face flushed from the raw spirits he had taken, stared at the two riders and waved a bottle in greeting.

'Jud! Sam! Step down and join us.'

'Are you mad!' Jud swung from his saddle and walked towards the squat man. 'What is this? No guards stationed, all the men drunk, what goes on?'

'We're leaving here, Jud, that's what goes on.' Brenhardt nodded towards the men. 'We got tired of sitting around doing nothing so I sent some of the boys into town to get some whiskey.' He held out his bottle. 'Here you are, Jud, take a swig.'

'No.' Jud swung his hand and knocked the bottle to the ground. The crash of glass brought a sudden silence and men, their faces ugly, began to move forward.

'Take it easy, Jud,' warned Brenhardt. 'Things are different now to what they were when you left. Some more of my boys rode in and we're having ourselves a party.'

'A party?' Jud stared his contempt. 'A drunken orgy more like it. Is this the way you keep order when Quantrill is away?'

'Forget Quantrill,' said Brenhardt. He looked down the pass. 'Where is he, anyway?'

'Dead.'

'And the others?'

'Dead.'

'Did you get the money?'

'We did.'

'Good.' Brenhardt chuckled, 'Well, that solves a problem. With Quantrill out of the way I take command. Relax and enjoy yourself, Jud.' He winked. 'That's orders.'

'I don't take orders from you,' said Jud quietly. 'With Quantrill dead I am next in command. Now get rid of that whiskey, damp down that fire, set guards and sober up. We may have the cavalry on us before we know it.' He stared at the squat man. 'You heard me, Brenhardt. Now move!'

'You've got things all wrong, Jud,' said Brenhardt easily. 'I don't think the boys will like playing at soldiers with you giving the orders. In fact, that wouldn't suit them at all.'

'No?'

'No.' Brenhardt grinned even wider. 'You see, Jud, we had a kind of election while you was away. These boys figure that they'd rather take orders from me than from you or Quantrill. In fact if Quantrill hadn't handed in his chips they might have acted a little rough towards him.' He winked. 'Get what I mean?'

Jud did. What had happened was obvious and, as he thought about it, he felt his stomach tighten and the muscle begin to twitch high on his cheek. Brenhardt had moved in his own men, the tough, lawless riders from over the border, outlaws, drifters, gunslingers who would kill a man for the sake of the boots he happened to be wearing. They had no loyalty, no obedience. They were human rats grabbing what they could get with no thought for tomorrow, a cause, or anything but lining their own pockets.

'So you had an election,' he said softly. 'What about our old riders?'

'We had to take care of them,' said Brenhardt. 'A couple of them even tried to kill me.' He shook his head. 'Too bad that I fired first.'

'So you killed them.' Jud took a deep breath. 'So you and I are the only original riders left and you were never one of Quantrill's men at heart.' He looked at the circle of men. 'What do you intend to do?'

'Can't you guess?' Brenhardt grinned again. 'First we collect all the money we can and head across the border. That million we collected will make a nice pile and we can use the Memphis money for small change. I guess that a man ought to be satisfied with a share in a million dollars, don't you? Maybe I'll buy myself a plantation in the south, they're going pretty cheap now, and set myself up as a local big shot. Maybe I'll even stand for election and get into the Senate.'

'You would do well there,' said Jud. 'Rats seem to get on well together.'

'Words don't hurt none,' said Brenhardt. 'Call me what you like, Jud, only don't go too far. I'm a patient man and I've no quarrel with you. Throw in with me and we'll both make out. Start something and we'll bury you with the others.' He grinned as he spoke but his hand dropped to his pistol and there was no mistaking the threat in his words. 'How about it, Jud? Do we act friendly or do we start shooting?'

'I've had enough shooting,' said Jud. 'And I'm tired. How about a drink of that whiskey?'

'Now you're talking.' Brenhardt snatched a bottle from a man and gave it to Jud. He pressed a second into Sam's hand and clapped both men on the shoulder. 'Join in the party you two, join in and have yourselves a time.'

Jud smiled and shook his head. 'I'm all in, Brenhardt. We've been riding for over a week without a decent rest. I'll grab a little sack-time and join in later.' He tilted the bottle and wiped his mouth with the back of his hand. 'Maybe we can have a little talk later. Just you and me and maybe Sam.'

'Sure, Jud.' Brenhardt glanced towards where the others had returned to their drinking and card playing. 'What about?'

'Figures,' said Jud easily. 'Take a million and divide it by twenty and it don't end so good. Divide it by three say, or maybe five, and it sounds a lot better.' He winked. 'Or am I wasting my time?'

'I'm ahead of you, Jud,' said Brenhardt. He grinned. 'Grab some rest and we'll talk about it.'

Jud nodded and, followed by Sam, walked towards one of the cabins.

It was deserted and smelt of tobacco smoke, stale whiskey and human sweat. Jud sniffed the air, snorted, and stood the bottle of whiskey on the table. They had their horses saddled, just as they had arrived, and the tired beasts were cropping the sparse grass which grew towards the opening of the pass. Jud stared at them from the window, then, turning, he looked at Sam.

'Well?'

'A nice picture,' said Sam. 'The end of Quantrill's Raiders. With Brenhardt in command he'll recruit every outlaw in the west and south. He'll ride at the head of a band which will operate worse than the Indians. He will rob and steal from every small town, stagecoach, and store he can reach. With his numbers he'll cut a path of terror through this country until they catch him and shoot him down like the mad dog he is.'

'You sound worried,' said Jud softly. 'Why?'

'Does it matter?' Sam realized that he had almost betrayed himself, not so much by what he said as the way in which he had said it. As an outlaw himself he should be glad that Brenhardt had taken over but, as the officer he was, he felt nothing but sick disgust at what would inevitably happen if the squat man rode at the head of this pack of human wolves.

'It could matter a lot,' said Jud. His hand dropped to his side. 'I've been wondering about you, Sam. I didn't like the way you joined us and, for a man who lives on the edge of the law you're a pretty bad shot.' Jud tensed as Sam's hand moved towards his gun. 'I've learned to recognize little things, Sam. The fact that a man never seems to kill an enemy, that he speaks different to what you'd expect, and that he could, possibly, be a spy.'

'Keep talking,' said Sam. His mouth felt dry and his stomach cramped with fear. If the big man should draw Sam knew that he would have no chance.

'We've always known that the Yankees might try to plant their own men among us,' continued Jud. 'That's why we were so careful in recruiting new riders.' His hand lifted from his side and Sam stared into the muzzle of a six-gun. The click as Jud thumbed back the hammer sounded very loud. 'Talk, Sam, and talk straight and fast. Who and what are you?'

'An officer of the United States,' said Sam. He looked directly at the big man. 'Kill me if you like but don't ever try to justify it. It would be murder and you know it.' He shrugged. 'During the war I suppose a case could be made out for Quantrill, he was an independent fighting for what he believed to be the right. But the war is over and any man who rides against peaceable citizens is an outlaw and no less and no better than the scum out

211

there!' He jerked his thumb towards the fire. 'It is the duty of every decent man, no matter where he was born, to stamp them out like the vermin they are.'

'Yes,' said Jud. 'Keep talking.'

'What else can I say? At a guess I'd say that you were an officer in the Confederate Army exactly as Quantrill was. As an officer you are a long way from rabble like Brenhardt. You swore to uphold the constitution and enforce the laws of the government. All right, then why don't you? Just because your side lost the war doesn't give you the right to justify acting like an owlhoot. Defeat never gives a man the right to act like a wolf. You should be against Brenhardt, not for him. To agree with what he says would make you as bad as he is.' Sam licked his lips as he stared at the tall man. 'I think I know you pretty well, Jud. You're not a bad man and I can understand you doing what you did. But that is in the past. Quantrill is dead. The South is defeated and the war is over. This is the end of the line. Follow Brenhardt and you will lose all self-respect.' Sam tilted his head at the sound of drunken laughter. 'Nice, isn't it? Not one of them feels sorry for the men we left lying dead on the ride from Memphis. Not one of them has any loyalty or decency. They are scum, Jud. Dogs. Do you want to become one of them?'

'I never reckoned that I would,' said the tall man mildly. He rested his thumb on the hammer of his Colt, pressed the trigger, eased the hammer back against the cartridge. He slipped the uncocked weapon back into its holster.

'Brenhardt is getting those men drunk for a reason. There's a million dollars in greenbacks in Quantrill's cabin and about fifty thousand in gold and other money. Brenhardt wants it for himself. He's picked four, maybe five men to ride with him and, when the rest are sodden with whiskey, they'll have themselves a slaughter. Unless we look after ourselves we will be lying with the dead.'

'We could hold back until he starts and then move in,' suggested Sam hopefully. Jud shook his head.

'Don't underestimate Brenhardt. He's bad and mean but he's no fool. He'll work it right all along the line. No, if we're going to escape and beat him we'll have to operate on our own.'

Jud stared out of the window to where the horses they had ridden, still saddled, cropped the grass at the end of the pass.

'We'll walk out of here, get on the horses, and ride down the pass. You can contact the military and tell them that Quantrill is dead.' He smiled. 'You might even get promotion for it. What are you, Sam?'

'A Captain.'

'So am I. A Captain without a uniform, an army, or a place to call his own. Hell, ain't it?'

Sam didn't answer. He had taken a chance and that chance had come off.

He had gambled his own knowledge of Jud's character against the possibility that he would be shot as a spy. Now it seemed that Jud was going to stamp out the nest of outlaws he had helped foster. Sam knew why. It was one thing to ride and to fight for a cause and with official approval. It was another to ride as an outlaw against decent, peace-loving men and women. The raid on Memphis with the cutting-down of innocent civilians, coupled with Brenhardt's treachery, had soured Jud's stomach.

'We'll walk slow and easy.' said Jud. 'Brenhardt will be watching us so don't seem to be in a hurry. We'll mount and ride.'

'The horses are jaded,' said Sam. 'They'd catch us before we'd gone a mile.'

'I'll attend to that,' said Jud. 'Ready? Let's go.'

Casually they sauntered from the cabin and moved around the edge of the clearing towards the end of the pass. It was growing dark, the tips of the twin peaks aflame with the light of the dying sun, and little pools of shadow helped to shield the two men as they moved towards the horses.

They had almost reached them when a man came blundering forwards.

'Hold it, rannies. Where you going?'

He was one of the new riders, stone sober, with twin guns hanging at his hips and narrowed, suspicious eyes.

'Walking,' said Jud. 'I — '

His hand as it moved was a blur but, as fast as he was, the gunslinger was almost as fast. Jud's Colt roared, to be answered with a stab of flame, then Jud fired again and the outlaw toppled, blood making his shirt an ugly mess.

'Mount,' said Jud thickly. 'Mount and ride!'

'Stop them!' Brenhardt came running towards the two men, his gun snarling after them. He turned and waved and a small bunch of outlaws ran for their horses. Sam thinned his lips as he felt his own mount falter beneath the spur.

'We'll never make it,' he said. 'The horses are about ready to drop.'

Jud didn't answer.

'You hear me?' Sam stared at the tall man. 'Jud, are you hurt?'

'A scratch.' Jud forced himself to smile and ignore the thick stream of warm wetness coursing down his side. He twisted in the saddle, reined, and dismounted. 'Give me your saddle-bags.'

'Why?'

'I want what's in them.' Jud grunted as he felt in the pouches and Sam swallowed as he recognized the waxen whiteness of dynamite.

'Take this money.' Jud swung the bags stuffed with bills to Sam's saddle. 'Right. Now ride slow and easy until you contact the military.'

'What about you?'

'Never mind about me.' Jud bit his lips as pain throbbed from his wound. 'Get going.'

'But — '

'Get moving!' Jud slapped the horse

on the flank and watched as it galloped away. Alone, he took his rifle from its scabbard, sent his own horse down the pass, and crouching behind a rock, primed and set a stick of dynamite. Lighting a cigar he rested the rifle before him and waited for the pursuit.

He didn't have long to wait.

A half-dozen mounted men came galloping down the pass, spurring their mounts and plying their quirts as they raced over the rocks between the peaks. Jud grunted, shot the first one from the saddle, sent the second flying for cover then, touching the tip of his cigar to the fuse, threw the stick of dynamite towards the rest.

They saw it coming, recognized it for what it was and jerked the reins as they turned and galloped back towards the clearing.

The explosion seemed to shake the very hills themselves.

Rocks cascaded down from the heights, heaping in the pass and making a low barrier from peak to peak. Jud, his face cut and bleeding from flying splinters of stone, stared up at the twin peaks, grunted as he saw a deep fissure in one and, moving with painful slowness, primed and fused the rest of the dynamite. Carefully he rammed the package deep into the fissure, unwound the fuse, and dropped behind a heap of rubble, his rifle pointing down the pass.

'Jud!' It was Brenhardt calling. 'You gone insane, Jud?'

'No.'

'What's the idea of dynamiting the pan?'

'Rats should be kept in their holes, Brenhardt,' said Jud. His voice sounded weak even to himself. 'I'm going to blow the peaks. I've enough giant powder to bring down enough rock to close this pass for always. You can stay here and be buried or get back and be safe.'

'You can't do that, we'd starve locked up in there.' Brenhardt sounded as if he couldn't believe it. 'Give up, Jud, we can share the money and live easy.'

Jud touched the end of his cigar to the fuse. It lit, throwing a little shower of sparks into the gathering darkness.

'You fool!' Rock splintered as lead whined against the stone. 'We'll rush you and put it out.'

'Try it.' Jud raised himself, stared down the sights of his rifle, and fired at a moving shadow. He missed, he hadn't expected anything else, but Brenhardt dived for shelter.

'Jud! Don't do it, man! Don't do it!'

'Ten seconds,' said Jud. 'I can hold you off that long.' He chuckled. 'The blast will be something to see, Brenhardt. I doubt if anything will be alive in the pass at all after it's over. Better get back to the clearing, Brenhardt, if you want to live.'

He smiled at the sound of hurried movement and the thudding of hooves as Brenhardt and his men, terrified of the coming explosion, ran for safety. Jud didn't run. He couldn't, his legs felt heavy and dead and he doubted if he could move them if he wanted to. He blinked, a little surprised that it was growing dark so soon and then, as he squinted at the fading speck of fire which was the burning fuse, he knew that the darkness was in his eyes and not the night.

He sighed, his thoughts flying like geese as the coldness crept higher around his body. Sam would contact the military and they would come to finish off the band of trapped outlaws. Quantrill's Raiders would die with Quantrill, their name and purpose unsullied by lesser men. He himself . . .

He sighed again, a long, deep sigh, and beneath him the rock seemed to become soft and warm and infinitely comfortable.

The fuse burned lower.

THE END

We do hope that you have enjoyed reading this large print book.

Did you know that all of our titles are available for purchase?

We publish a wide range of high quality large print books including:
Romances, Mysteries, Classics
General Fiction
Non Fiction and Westerns

Special interest titles available in large print are:
The Little Oxford Dictionary
Music Book, Song Book
Hymn Book, Service Book

Also available from us courtesy of Oxford University Press:
Young Readers' Dictionary
(large print edition)
Young Readers' Thesaurus
(large print edition)

For further information or a free brochure, please contact us at:
Ulverscroft Large Print Books Ltd.,
The Green, Bradgate Road, Anstey,
Leicester, LE7 7FU, England.
Tel: (00 44) **0116 236 4325**
Fax: (00 44) **0116 234 0205**

Other titles in the
Linford Western Library:

RIDE BACK TO REDEMPTION

Eugene Clifton

After a bank raid robbed him of his wife and unborn child, Jeff Warrinder, sheriff of Redemption, ended up a drunken no-hoper. Working off a debt to Cassie Hanson, he gets tangled up in her feud with Bull Krantz. Meanwhile, the new sheriff is in deep trouble, whilst Krantz's gang of outlaws is after Jeff's blood. If he's ever to make the ride back to Redemption, Jeff must overcome his own demon: the one that comes in a whisky bottle.

MARSHAL LAW

Corba Sunman

Deputy Marshal Jed Law was sent to Buffalo Crossing to keep the peace; a bloody feud between two ranchers had already cost a man his life. But Law's real troubles started when he first set eyes on Julie Rutherford and her father Ben . . . Opposed by hard cases determined to wipe him out, he would be forced to shoot his way through. And worse was to come . . . Law would need his pistol loaded and ready to use until the last desperate shot.

HOT LEAD RANGE

Jack Holt

When an undercover agent going by the name of Bob Harker arrives in Sweetwater Valley, his task is to prevent a range war developing: the ruthless Butch Collins intends to claim the entire valley by forcing out his neighbours. One such neighbour is Frank Bateman — Harker's old boss when he was a Pinkerton detective. Harker manages to infiltrate the Collins outfit but, forced to take ever greater risks, could this be his final mission?

BADLANDERS

Ben Nicholas

The mining town of Sundown was running into chaos. When the sheriff faltered and shots sounded, hardcase miners took to the streets — fired up and ready for a showdown with anyone who stood in their way. Shane Carson was waiting for them at the jailhouse. Carson was no lawman, but he was a man on a mission — even if that meant standing alone against a murderous rabble. But could anybody hope to stand against such odds and live?